**“What is it tha[illegible]**
**Bowie?”**

*You.* A half dozen kids—bio, foster, adopted, he didn’t care.

But Bowie said, “I have everything a man could want, except my own family, I suppose. Not that I’m complaining. My life is good. But I don’t want to be a bachelor forever.”

The recent wedding and forever stuff had wiggled its way into his head.

Sage nodded slowly, those Mountain Dew eyes still holding him. “I can see you married, with a family. You’re such a stable guy and great with kids. You’re the marrying kind, Bowie Trudeau.”

His heart set up a thundering pace, squeezing with a hope he quickly repressed. “What about you, Sage? Can you see yourself married with kids? Are you the marrying kind?”

She dropped her attention to the sprawling home he wanted to build someday, quiet for long, aching moments in which he wished he hadn’t asked.

“Someday. Maybe. When I’m ready to grow roots. When the right man comes along.”

And there he had his answer.

**Linda Goodnight**, a *New York Times* bestselling author and winner of a RITA® Award in inspirational fiction, has appeared on the Christian bestseller list. Her novels have been translated into more than a dozen languages. Active in orphan ministry, Linda enjoys writing fiction that carries a message of hope in a sometimes dark world. She and her husband live in Oklahoma. Visit her website, lindagoodnight.com, for more information.

**Books by Linda Goodnight**

**Love Inspired**

***Sundown Valley***

*To Protect His Children*
*Keeping Them Safe*

***The Buchanons***

*Cowboy Under the Mistletoe*
*The Christmas Family*
*Lone Star Dad*
*Lone Star Bachelor*

***Whisper Falls***

*Rancher's Refuge*
*Baby in His Arms*
*Sugarplum Homecoming*
*The Lawman's Honor*

Visit the Author Profile page at LoveInspired.com for more titles.

# Keeping Them Safe

## Linda Goodnight

ISBN-13: 978-1-335-75918-4

Keeping Them Safe



This edition published by arrangement with Harlequin Books S.A.

For questions and comments about the quality of this book, please contact us at CustomerService@Harlequin.com.

Love Inspired
22 Adelaide St. West, 41st Floor
Toronto, Ontario M5H 4E3, Canada
www.LoveInspired.com

**Printed in U.S.A.**

Remember ye not the former things,
neither consider the things of old. Behold,
I will do a new thing; now it shall spring forth;
shall ye not know it?

—*Isaiah* 43:18–19

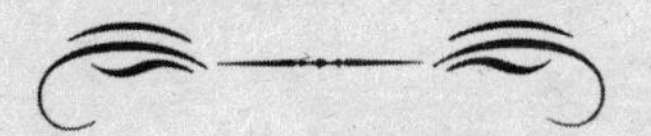

In memory of my son, Travis,
and with gratitude to my Lord Jesus for the
hope I have of one day spending forever
with him…and Him…where time has no end
and cancer is no more.

# *Chapter One*

She was pretty sure kidnapping was a federal offense. Or did that only count if the kids in question were strangers?

This worry nagged Sage Walker something fierce the evening she drove into Sundown Valley, Oklahoma, the town she'd sworn never to see again. But anytime she said *never*, life would laugh out loud and then force her to do that very thing. She'd learned from experience that the world had a way of kicking you when you're down.

So here she was, back in the small Kiamichi Mountain town, hoping and praying that Ms. Bea would take them in for a few days until she could figure out where else to go.

"Please understand," she prayed under her breath.

Considering her actions of the past couple of days, the good Lord probably wasn't even listening.

"What?" Ryder, her eight-year-old nephew, unsnapped his seatbelt for the tenth time and leaned between the seats. "What did you say?"

"I was praying."

"Oh."

"Please sit back, Ryder. And buckle up."

He sat back, but Sage didn't hear the buckle click. With a beleaguered sigh, she slowed the car, pulled into a convenience store driveway and stopped, turning her head to look into the back seat.

Ryder's eyes met hers. "Mama doesn't make me."

Sage wasn't opening *that* can of worms. His mama

didn't make him do a lot of things. Like go to school on a regular basis.

"Put on your seat belt, please. I want you to be safe."

Paisley, the silent, big-eyed four-year-old watched the mental wrestling match with concern and clutched her scrap of a security blanket against her cheek in a death grip.

Ryder glared, rebellious, for a full fifteen seconds before reaching for the belt. When the satisfactory snick sounded, Sage pulled back onto the road and aimed the car toward Main Street, hoping the bakery was still open. The kids hadn't eaten, and if Ms. Bea was at the shop she'd fill them with leftovers.

At least that's what she would have done in years past. In Sage's mind, Ms. Bea was not allowed to change, though it had been nearly thirteen years since their last face-to-face meeting. Shame would do that to a person.

Sage squinted a doubtful eye at the clock on the Jeep's dash. It was almost six, closing time at the Bea Sweet Bakery.

She suffered a grinding twist of guilt that her phone calls to her former foster mom had become so sporadic that she knew next to nothing about Ms. Bea—or the Bea Sweet Bakery—anymore.

She should have called before leaving Kansas City, but she'd been afraid to. Of what, exactly, she wasn't sure, but she was taking no chances. Not with the kids in tow.

They'd needed to get out of Missouri fast.

Main Street came into sight. Though it was still light outside, darkness arrived early this time of year, and the streetlights had already come on. The diagonal parking spaces outside most businesses were empty. The stores were closed or in the process of locking up. That much, at least, hadn't changed.

Sundown Valley rolled up the streets early, so only convenience stores and a few eating places remained open past six. She wondered if the town was big enough yet for any big box stores? She hadn't seen any driving in.

Lights remained on at the bakery but the only vehicle parked outside was an oversize silver-and-black pickup, the kind of four-wheel drive vehicle driven by ranchers in the area. Those fortunate souls with a little jingle in their pockets.

As she pulled in beside the truck, a well-built cowboy in crisp new blue jeans, gleamingly polished boots and a white dress shirt removed a tool belt and tossed it into the back. Though his shirt was tieless and unbuttoned at the top, he wasn't exactly dressed to be a handyman.

Unable to see his face, Sage didn't know if she recognized Mr. Tool Belt, but he was taller than she was. In a town as small as Sundown Valley, not many were.

Before she could stare at the cowboy another second, Ryder had his seat belt off, had unbuckled Paisley's and was out of the car yanking on the glass entry into the bakery.

The boy was like a caged pup and she couldn't blame him. All those hours in a car had taken a toll on her. She was sure the kids were exhausted from the long drive and needed to stretch their legs.

"I'm hungry." Holding Paisley's hand, Ryder barreled into the shop.

Not knowing how the kids would behave, Sage dragged her attention from the stranger to her niece and nephew and hurried inside too.

The smell hit her first. So familiar and fragrant, the sweet, yeasty scents she'd forever associate with home and love, though she'd only lived with Ms. Bea and Mr. Ron for four years.

Ms. Bea exited the kitchen area, dish towel over one shoulder. She'd aged. The once spritely baker now shuffled like a woman with painful knees or feet. Those weren't something a caller could see on a video chat, and, not surprisingly, Ms. Bea had never said a word.

When Bea spotted Sage, she stopped, blinked twice, and then broke into a smile. "Sage, honey, is that you?"

"It's me, Ms. Bea." To save the other woman from the effort of coming to her, Sage hurried behind the glass display counter for a welcome hug.

The older woman's plump, fleshy arms, warm as sunshine, enveloped her. When was the last time anyone had hugged her with real feeling? As if they actually cared for her?

And wasn't she being pitiful today?

She, who'd made her own way most of her life, who'd battled back from the brink of destruction more than once, who knew how to stiffen her spine and get on with life, refused to feel sorry for herself. Most of her troubles were of her own making.

Except for this time.

She cleared her too-full throat and stepped back. "You still give the best hugs in the world."

"Oh, honey, it's so good to see you. Let me look at you." Ms. Bea held her at arm's length, this caring woman who was nearly a foot shorter and half a body wider gazed at her with genuine affection in lively brown eyes.

Sage didn't want Ms. Bea or anyone else to look too deeply. A lot of miles had passed and a lot of mistakes had been made since she'd last eaten in the Bea Sweet.

"You're still the prettiest thing I've ever laid eyes on. After you left, Ron and I used to talk about that. You'd be a big success out there in the Big Apple with all your tall green-eyed beauty."

Another shot of guilt. "I should have been here when Mr. Ron passed. I'm sorry."

Bea waved a hand, though those sparkling brown eyes grew sad. "It was fast, honey. One minute my Ron was in the kitchen frying doughnuts and the next he was gone. That's the way he wanted to go, doing what he loved most, and the good Lord saw fit to let him have his wish."

Still, she should have come. But again, shame had kept

her away. Shame, no money and being in a place that would shock the godly, wholesome and decidedly old-fashioned Ms. Bea to the tips of her flour-coated fingers.

"I hope you don't mind the unannounced visit."

"Any way I can get a visit from you is fine with me." Bea's kind gaze moved to the children. "These little darlings must be Amy's babies?"

Ryder and Paisley stood in front of the display cases, faces pressed against the glass, expressions clearly stating their desire for every kind of sweet pastry in the building.

"Yes." Sage put a hand on each child's shoulder. "This is Ryder and this is Paisley. Kids, this is Ms. Bea. She raised your mama and me."

Or tried to.

Kids, as inclined to do, cast a quick look at the baker and returned to drooling over the day's remaining pastries.

Ms. Bea chuckled. "I think they're hungry." Taking control as she'd done with many foster children, including Sage and Amy, she guided the duo toward the back of the bakery. "You can choose anything you want after we get something nourishing in you."

Ms. Bea was still the same nurturing, motherly soul, and her kindness warmed a cold place in Sage's middle. She'd been cold for days. Maybe here she could get warm again.

She'd needed this. Needed the assurance that someone on this planet still cared.

"Thank you, Ms. Bea," she said as the kids and Bea disappeared into the back.

She was about to follow when the bell over the door jingled and the tall cowboy entered.

"Ms. Bea—" he started but the words died on his lips as his very dark brown gaze fell on her. Thick, spiky black lashes blinked at her. "Sage?"

"Bowie? Bowie Trudeau?"

"Long time," he said, his voice velvety soft the way she remembered.

No wonder he'd looked familiar. The oldest three Trudeau men were all taller than her, and Bowie was the tallest. He'd always been the quiet, steady Trudeau while the others had been rowdy and sometimes a little wild.

Sweet memories unfurled beneath her breastbone. She wondered if Bowie was still everybody's best friend? He'd been hers.

Shifting on his expensive boots, a slight darkening on his already-dark cheekbones, Bowie asked, "You doing okay?"

"Just dandy." If you could call running from authorities dandy. But then she'd always been the rebel, and Bowie knew it as well as anyone. Or he had back in the day. Sweet, kindhearted Bowie. "You?"

"Good. I'm looking for Ms. Bea."

Bowie had never been a big talker. Apparently, that hadn't changed.

Just then, Bea shuffled through the doorway leading from the back kitchen area.

"I thought I heard your voice," she said to Bowie. "Did you forget something?"

"Yes, ma'am. I've got to run to the city in the morning, but I'll stop by tomorrow evening and check that hot water heater again to be sure it's still working properly."

Ms. Bea flapped a hand. "Now, don't you give that another thought. It's bad enough I dragged you away from Wade's wedding. I imagine it was beautiful."

"Real pretty. Your cake was good too." A dazzling grin accented the dimple in his chin. "I ate two pieces."

Ms. Bea's wrinkles softened into a pleased smile. "I don't make many wedding cakes anymore, but you Trudeau boys are special. You'd better hurry up and settle down yourself before I'm too old to bake yours."

Bowie's grin just widened. He started out again, pausing only to touch the brim of his hat and say, "Nice to see you again, Sage."

Before she could ask about Wade's wedding or any of

the other Trudeaus, Bowie slipped out the door and ambled with long, easy strides to his truck.

Sage realized, then, that she was staring and that the tall, shy boy she'd known in high school had grown into a gorgeous, kindhearted man who probably made a few hearts in this town flutter.

And he wasn't yet married.

Interesting. Not for her, of course. They'd been buddies, nothing more, but Bowie was definitely a catch.

What was wrong with the women of this town?

Sage Walker was back in Sundown Valley.

Bowie aimed his truck toward home. It had been a long day, a good one filled with love and people and a beautiful wedding, but he was eager for some solitude in his workshop.

Running into Sage Walker had shaken him. It had also shot a bolus of energy through his bloodstream stronger than a can of Red Bull.

"Sage," he murmured to the air freshener dangling from his rearview mirror, a joke from Wade's new wife after he'd tracked cow manure into the bunkhouse where she'd lived for the last year. The freshener smelled like his favorite cologne so he'd left it hanging there.

But it was Sage he was thinking about, not the air freshener. Somebody at his cousin's wedding earlier today said they'd seen her at a gas station outside of town. After his initial shocked reaction, he considered it a case of mistaken identity.

"What's she doing in Sundown Valley after all these years?"

Straight out of high school, she'd left to take the modeling world by storm. He'd looked online a few times in hopes of seeing her, but whatever she'd done in New York, she'd kept a low profile. Not that he was into social media all that much. He was too busy.

Back in the day, she'd easily been the prettiest girl in

Sundown Valley High School, especially to a shy, gangly teenage boy with a big crush.

Now, her youthful beauty had blossomed and Sage was even more stunningly beautiful today than then, a beauty who nearly stole a man's breath right out of his lungs. Tall, shapely and graceful with sleek black hair down her back, the palest green eyes on earth and a perfect face, she was an artist's dream. He'd tried to paint her once, but his talent lay elsewhere. No one knew about the painting except him.

Although he was no longer gangly or all that shy, he'd gone tongue-tied the minute he'd recognized her. He, a grown man of thirty-two, still let Sage Walker make his heart jump.

She'd never known, of course, never had an inkling. He was her buddy, her best friend, her shoulder to cry on.

But that was a long time ago.

He was a man now and he knew better. Sage was a walk-away Joe. Or in her case, a runaway with a heart as restless as an Oklahoma wind.

He liked people, enjoyed a date now and then, but putting his heart out there was not going to happen. At least, not with Sage.

Though why he was even thinking this way bothered him.

Turning off the highway leading out of town, he followed a gravel road that wound up and around a low mountain toward the sprawling ranch he owned with his cousins, Wade and Yates Trudeau. Except Yates, like Sage, had been gone for a long time. He hadn't even bothered to attend his younger brother's wedding.

The neglect had hurt Wade, which in turn hurt Bowie. He'd do about anything for the men he considered brothers. Daily, he asked the Lord to mend the brokenness between Wade and Yates and to bring the oldest brother home to the Sundown. Like Wade, he shot off texts and made calls that invariably ended in voice mails, rarely connecting with the mysteriously absent Yates.

Family troubles. Bowie hated them. Had his fill of them. Like Wade, he was helpless to change any of it. He hadn't seen his own mother since she'd left him at a shelter in New Orleans at the age of ten.

If not for the kind folks in that shelter, he'd never have ended up here on the Sundown.

He rubbed a hand over the back of his neck. Today was a day of celebration. Wade had married a wonderful woman who loved his three babies and her new husband with a love that anyone could see if they had eyes. Bowie had no business digging up old, buried bones and getting melancholy.

No one should feel low in autumn, his favorite season, when God's glory flamed the hills and valleys, the hay harvest was in for the winter, and cooler temperatures made outdoor work and play enjoyable.

He had a good life, thanks to the aunt and uncle who'd not only taken him in, they'd made him a joint heir with his cousins. Regardless of the aloneness that sometimes plagued him, he had no right to complain.

Heather and Brett Trudeau had accepted him with open arms and hearts when the shelter had contacted them. For all they knew, he wasn't a Trudeau at all. But the woman who'd birthed him claimed he was the son of Brian Lee Trudeau, Brett's late brother, and that was good enough for Brett and Heather.

They'd given him a home, a family, love and an equal share of the Sundown Ranch. Most importantly, they'd given him a faith in Jesus. Though he'd strayed a few times, messed up, failed, he prayed they'd never known. He owed them too much, had loved them too deeply to hurt them. Not after they'd taken in a stray and made him their own.

It wasn't their fault he still thought of himself as an

outsider, the odd man out, who didn't quite fit. Heather and Brett had done their best. He was the one with the baggage he'd never been able to shed, though they hadn't known. At least, he hoped they hadn't. He wouldn't hurt them for the world.

Sometimes he still got misty-eyed, missing them, wondering why good people seemed to die early and the bad ones were left. But he was a man who trusted that the Lord knew what He was doing even if humans didn't.

His was a simple faith. Trust Jesus, be good to people and everything else would work out.

Once or twice after Brett and Heather died, he'd considered striking out on his own, accomplishing something for himself by himself. He never had.

After Yates took off, he couldn't have left no matter how much he might have wanted to. Wade needed him. He and his cousin were the only ones remaining to run the Sundown and carry on Brett and Heather's legacy. He owed them too much to leave, then or now.

So he'd remained. And he'd learned, as the Bible directed, to be content.

When the ranch's main house came into sight, lights blazed from the windows. Mrs. Roberta, the widowed, part-time nanny Wade had hired last year was in charge of the triplets while the newlyweds took a honeymoon. Bowie would check in on the babies tomorrow and every day thereafter, but the grandmotherly Roberta would hold down the fort and call him if she needed him. Tonight, he needed time in his workshop, time to untangle the day's worries, to talk to Jesus, and create something beautiful with his hands. Lately, he'd found little time for his art, his passion.

He had a bunk in the shop if he wanted to spend the night and tonight, he wanted to.

Now that Wade and Kyra were married and she'd moved her things into the main house, maybe it was time for him to move out of the main house for good. They hadn't asked him to, didn't expect him to, but they were a growing family and he was a third wheel.

He'd always intended to build his own house someday. He'd started making plans a few times, but the cattle market would take a dip, and he'd worry about finances. Supporting the New Orleans mission that had saved his life was more important than building a house for himself.

There was always the bunkhouse. He could move his belongings out there now that Kyra had made it livable, if a little girly for his tastes. She didn't need it anymore. It was plenty good enough for a single cowboy with minimal needs.

Yet, the idea of being alone, totally alone, brought on the empty gnawing in his belly. He loved the noise and togetherness of family. Unlike his old mountain man friend, Jinx Vanderbilt, he was not a loner.

Pulling his truck up next to the long metal building he'd built as a workshop, he parked. A security light glowed yellowish white above the door. Exiting the truck, he went to the door and unlocked it.

In the country quiet, he heard a rustling sound and paused to look around. The ranch sometimes had issues with the neighboring Keno family, a father and sons who bore some kind of grudge against anyone named Trudeau. Bowie never had figured out why, but he'd learned to keep his eyes peeled for trouble.

He wouldn't put it past one of the Kenos to cause trouble today when they'd likely heard that Wade was off on his honeymoon and Bowie was the only Trudeau on site.

Seeing nothing near the front, he opened the flashlight app on his cell phone and walked around the building. His favorite horse, Diesel, whickered a greeting from the nearby pasture. Otherwise the night was still.

As he stood in the deepening darkness, watching the moon rise over the mountain, thinking about today's wedding and how happy he was for his cousin, the noise came again.

Frowning, he circled the building and then went inside, flipping the lights on to cautiously scan the interior. Nothing seemed out of place.

Birds? Bats? Rats? This was country. Could have been any kind of critter.

Shaking off the episode, Bowie went to his workbench and took up the leather wallet he'd begun crafting days ago. He'd been so busy with Wade's wedding preparations, ranch work and helping widowed friends that he'd not had time for this. He'd missed it.

Working the soft leather, inventing designs and crafting usable products gave him a sense of satisfaction he got nowhere else.

His cell phone pinged. Frustrated at another interruption, he nonetheless slid the device from his back pocket and read the text message, concerned it could be Mrs. Roberta or Wade.

Expect a call from a friend of mine, a big-time buyer. I showed her the things you made for us. She was especially impressed with Angi's purse and is interested in seeing more.

Bowie frowned in thought at the message, pondering his Colorado friend's words. Jim and Angi ran an Aspen resort, and, as such, knew many highly successful people. Like big-time buyers and investors.

Bowie's pulse hit double time. Did this mean what he thought it meant? That his dream of doing more than hobby work with his leather craft could become a reality?

He shot a quick text in reply.

A big-time buyer of what?

I don't have details. Just a contact for you. Expect a call tomorrow.

He wouldn't get his hopes up too high, but he would be waiting for that phone call.

After allowing a momentary thrill to filter through him, Bowie picked up the wallet and got back to work.

The smell and feel of supple new leather filled his senses as he took up a swivel knife and began to carve the horse head design into the leather. He forgot that he hadn't eaten. Forgot that he'd been the best man at his cousin's wedding. Forgot even that Sage Walker was back in town. As he always did, Bowie got lost in his art.

When he heard someone sneeze, he had to shake his head to decide if the sound was real or imaginary. Blinking around at the long workshop, he saw no one. But someone had to be in here.

A charge, like electricity, shot down his spine. "If that's one of you Keno boys, come out and show yourself. I'm on to you."

Nothing stirred.

"Who's in here?" He began a search.

Though the only other walled room in the building was a bathroom and he kept his shop tidy, there was a storage cabinet beneath the sink, a huge tool chest and two tall metal cabinets a person could hide behind or, possibly, inside. There was also the bunk he slept in, though none of the robust Kenos would fit under there.

Taking a cobbler's hammer in hand, Bowie searched the shop, coming up empty. Just when he'd decided he'd imagined the sneeze, he heard a rustling sound, as if someone had moved but was trying not to make noise.

It came from his bunk.

Crouching low, hammer ready, he peered under the bed.

Two pairs of eyes, wide and frightened, stared back at him.

Two kids. A boy and a girl. Very young. What in the world were they doing in his shop? How had they gotten here? The only kids he knew out here in the country were Wade's triplets.

The little girl began to snivel. The boy wiggled until he could get a hand on her shoulder. "Shh, sissy, it's okay."

Something in the boy's protectiveness toward the little girl touched a bruised place in Bowie's chest.

He put the hammer aside and lay flat on his belly the way the children were. "Come on out. I won't hurt you."

The boy hesitated, uncertain, untrusting. Bowie waited, quiet and easy as he would with a skittish colt. He could practically smell the boy's anxiety, understood it and waited, letting the child call the shots.

The little girl whispered something Bowie couldn't hear. The boy sighed and crawled out, turning to assist the girl.

"You got a bathroom?" he asked. "My sister needs to go. She don't wait real good."

Bowie escorted them to the bathroom and took note that the boy stood outside the door like a guard.

Dipping a shoulder against the wall adjacent to the bathroom, he intentionally struck a relaxed pose in hopes of putting the boy at ease. "What's your name, buddy?"

The little boy swallowed and looked away, arms stiff at his sides. The kid was scared, but he had grit. His sister was inside that bathroom, and he wasn't budging from his post.

"I'm Bowie Trudeau. You can call me Bowie. This is my shop. Want to tell me what you're doing out here alone?"

He heard the toilet flush and water run. Then the little girl came out and huddled behind her brother, a plush cloth against her face. Bowie recognized the type of security blanket the triplets called their "lovey," only this one had a fluffy white lamb's head at one end.

Bowie crouched in front of her. "What's your name, little one?"

The boy used his slender body to block his sister from Bowie. "She's only four. She won't talk to you."

But she talked to her brother.

"How old are you?"

"Eight."

Too young to be out here alone. "Where were you headed when you ended up in my workshop?"

"Home."

"Tell me where that is, and I'll take you there. Sundown Valley? Or out here in the country somewhere?"

The boy looked confused. He blinked, his eyelashes touched his overlong bangs. "The city."

The city? That didn't make any sense. "How did you get here?"

The boy didn't answer. With a sigh, Bowie racked his brain. What was he supposed to do with two stray kids?

The moment the word *stray* entered his head, he slapped it down. Kids were not strays. He, of all people, should know that. Feeling like a stray wasn't good for anyone. He also knew that from experience.

His belly rumbled, and it occurred to him to ask, "Are you hungry?"

The boy shrugged. "My sister is."

Which meant he was too.

Bowie went to the small dorm-size refrigerator that served his needs and took out sandwich fixings.

"Ham and cheese okay?" he asked as he placed a plate on the wall-mounted counter that held both the fridge and microwave for those times when he wasn't in the mood to go to the main house to eat. He lined the plate with bread slices.

"Thanks, mister."

"Bowie." He handed the kid a sandwich. "Sure you

won't tell me your name? It would help me find where you belong."

"Ryder."

Now they were getting somewhere.

Ryder handed his sandwich to the girl and waited. The piercingly sweet gesture moved Bowie to rummage around in his storage cabinet for a half bag of Cheetos closed with a rubber band and three bottles of water which he toted to the long wooden bench next to his worktable.

When they'd gobbled down their sandwiches, and their fingers were orange from the chips, Ryder wiped his hands down his jeans and looked around the shop.

"Is this your place?"

"Yes. My workshop."

"Do you live here?" He aimed his gaze toward the corner bunk.

"No. Sometimes I work late, though, and don't want to drive home."

The boy pointed toward his work area and the leather piece lying across the tooling stone. "What are you making?"

"A wallet."

"I didn't know people could make a wallet."

"How did you think they came into existence?" Maybe that was too complicated a question for a boy of eight.

Curious brown eyes, darker than the boy's sandy hair, moved from the worktable to Bowie. "Can I look?"

"Yes, but I'd rather you didn't touch until you wash your hands."

Ryder glanced down at his orange fingertips and said, "Oh."

With his sister in tow, the boy hustled into the bathroom and returned with clean, damp hands to stand next to Bowie at his workbench.

Bowie didn't know much about kids this age. His relationship with children was limited to his cousin's two-and-a-half-year-old triplets. Somehow he had to get these two talking and figure out where they belonged. If they didn't speak up soon, he'd have to call the sheriff. For some reason, he didn't want to do that, though the county sheriff was a good guy.

He figured it stemmed from those childhood days in New Orleans when street people scattered at the sight of a cop.

"Do you like horses?" In his book, horses were one of those topics everyone likes, a natural conversation starter.

"I never saw one in real life."

"You've never seen a horse?"

"Uh-uh. Just on TV."

Well now, that was just real sad. If it was daylight, he'd take the kid out and introduce him to Chigger, the sweetest old horse on the place.

"This is pretty." The boy pointed to the horse's head and neck Bowie had been carving into the leather.

Bowie let him feel the leather and then demonstrated a carving technique. The boy was surprisingly attentive for a little guy, though he kept a watch on his sister.

The tiny girl had plopped down on the floor at her brother's feet and leaned her head against his shoe, clinging to his leg with one hand while she clutched her lovey with the other.

Slowly, like settling a wild horse, Bowie thought he was winning the boy's trust.

After a few minutes, he casually hitched his chin toward the little girl. "Your sister's sleepy."

Ryder glanced down and then up at Bowie. "Can we sleep in here tonight? I got money to pay you."

He dug in his jeans pocket and extracted a dime and four pennies.

Bowie's heart clutched. He reached out and curled the boy's fingers over the coins. "Keep your money, Ryder. You might need it. I'll get you home to your family. They'll be worried about you."

"You said you was going to the city tomorrow. Can me and Paisley ride with you?"

Bowie blinked. "How do you know that?"

The boy clammed up again.

Weeding through his brain cells, Bowie tried to recall when he'd told anyone about his plans to make the long drive to Oklahoma City.

"You were at the bakery, weren't you? You heard me tell Ms. Bea that I was going to the city tomorrow."

He hadn't seen any kids, but they must have either been in Ms. Bea's kitchen or somewhere on the sidewalk nearby.

And they must have hitched a ride in the back of his truck, under the tarp he kept there for wrapping sick calves.

The next thought hit him like a baseball bat to the head. Did Sage have kids? She was fresh into town, and last he'd heard, she lived in a city. Even though he'd seen no signs of children, she'd been at the bakery.

But if these were her kids, why had they run away? Why did they appear shaggy and unkempt?

"Tell you what, Ryder. You and your sister come with me into town, and we'll figure this whole thing out." To sweeten the deal, he added, "I'll buy you an ice cream cone."

The girl, Paisley, popped up from the floor, her big brown eyes round as silver dollars. She nodded at her brother with the most animation he'd seen from her since discovering them under his bunk.

It was settled. Back into town he'd go. If they weren't Sage's kids, Ms. Bea might know who they were.

No matter who they belonged to, he wanted some answers.

What had compelled two such young children to run away?

# *Chapter Two*

Frantic, scared, and out of options, Sage paused in the back alley behind the drug store to catch her breath. She'd run all the way down Main Street to the Sonic drive-in and back up through the alleyways searching for the kids.

No sign of them anywhere.

"Where are you?" she puffed, heart banging like the drums at a rock concert.

Normally a long run didn't bother her, but this was different. She was running on fear.

Hand against the catch in her side, she leaned against a big green trash receptacle. She was not one to panic easily, but she'd about reached her limit.

Night had fallen. It was now dark. The kids had never been in this town. They didn't know a soul. They had no money, no cell phone.

*Dear God in Heaven, keep them safe. I've messed up so many things in my life. Don't let me mess them up too.*

After making one more desperate survey of the alley, she started back to the bakery.

Ms. Bea met her at the back door. Worry wreathed her face. "Did you find them?"

Sage shook her head as she came inside and collapsed at the tiny two-person bistro table near the exit door. She remembered eating lunch in this very spot during summer break in high school.

Elbow on the table, forehead to her palm, she moaned, "Where could they have gone, Ms. Bea?"

Ms. Bea patted her hair. "I don't know, but it's time to call Adam Granger. You remember him, don't you?"

Sage straightened, puzzled.

"I think so. Short, strong guy with blond hair? He was a couple of years ahead of me in school." Though what Adam Granger had to do with finding the kids, she didn't know.

"Adam's the police chief now." Moving slowly and painfully, Bea started for the phone, a landline connected to the wall between the kitchen and the public area. "He's a good man. He'll come running."

"No!"

When Ms. Bea's head whipped back around, eyes wide with question, Sage tempered her objection. "What I mean is, we should give them a little more time to come back. They're probably just—" she waved a hand, searching for a reason, any reason, why two small children would be running around alone in a strange town "—exploring. Ryder is street smart. He'll watch out for Paisley."

But he was little too.

"Well," Ms. Bea looked doubtful, "if you're sure."

She wasn't.

"Let's just…wait a few more minutes." What she really wanted to do was to go screaming all over town, pounding on doors until Ryder and Paisley reappeared. She also didn't want the police involved. "A policeman might scare them."

They'd had plenty of negative experiences with police, none of which was the fault of law enforcement, nor the kids.

She glanced at the time on her cell phone. She'd give them five more minutes. If they weren't back by then, she'd have no choice.

She didn't even want to think what would happen if she had to call the police.

Would she go to jail? If she did, what would happen to the kids?

Needing to expend nervous energy, Sage went into the front of the shop to the bakery's small eat-in area and peered out the plate glass window. Bea Sweet Bakery scrolled across her line of vision in white cursive above a stenciled plate of sweet rolls and a steaming cup of coffee. A paper poster taped in one corner proclaimed a fifth Sunday singing at Praise Temple.

The poster reminded her to pray.

"Father in Heaven, please keep them safe. Please." *Where are they?*

Across the street, the stores were visible under streetlights but there was no sign of two small children.

Her head started to pound. She pressed it against the cool window glass and prayed again, her mind too jittery to do much except repeat, *keep them safe, keep them safe.*

When she heard Ms. Bea shuffle out from the kitchen, Sage turned. The older woman toted two cups of coffee and a plate of leftover bear claws. She placed them on one of the tables and, with a heavy sigh, sank into the chair as if her legs could no longer hold her.

"Sit down, Sage, and tell me what's going on. What's wrong? Why do you have Amy's kids?"

She should have known Ms. Bea would have questions. Bea Cunningham was a smart woman, wise about the ways of the world after running a small family business and caring for foster children most of her adult life.

The lump in her chest so hard and tight Sage thought she might choke, she scraped the opposite chair away from the table and sat across from her former foster mom, the only person resembling a real mother she could remember.

"Amy's in trouble again." *Again* being the key word. Amy had been in and out of trouble most of her life.

Bea pinched off a bite of bear claw. "I gathered as much from our last few phone calls. What happened this time?"

Sage pressed her lips together, fidgeted with the infinity ring on her finger. Amy owned an identical ring engraved inside with the simple phrase *Sisters are forever.*

Sage had had it engraved one Christmas to let Amy know she would be there for her no matter what.

She hadn't expected that promise to be so hard to keep. But she was all the family Amy had besides those two innocent kids.

"Drugs. Shoplifting. Burglary." The truth was hard to admit to this woman who'd done her best to teach the Walker sisters right from wrong. "I'm taking care of Ryder and Paisley until she's out of jail."

That was the truth, though not all of it.

Bea's hand went to her heart. "Jail? Oh, honey."

"Amy started running with the wrong people, Ms. Bea, and they burglarized houses to feed their habits. She got caught."

It wasn't her first offense.

Though she was already too jittery for coffee, Sage paused and took a sip, grief-stricken that she was to blame for her sister's problems.

Talking about it hurt, but she forced the words out. "Everything's a mess. Amy's in jail for who knows how long. The kids haven't been in school in a while. My job ended last week, but I had to take the kids. They needed me. I didn't know what else to do."

She'd left out half the story, but that's the way it had to be for now.

Sympathetic eyes held hers. "So you came home to Sundown Valley."

"I came home to *you*, Ms. Bea."

Bea patted the top of her hand. "You can stay right here as long as you need to. You and the babies. I'll tell you what else. We're going to pray the house down for our Amy. That's what we'll do. The Lord can straighten her out."

Sage knew that was true. He could. If Amy would let Him.

A fledgling sprout of relief moved into the room. She'd hoped for this, prayed for this, but after all the time away, she'd been uncertain.

"We won't be a burden, I promise. While we're here, I'll find some kind of work and pay you room and board." But what kind of job would hire someone who had no idea how long they'd be in town? Maybe a few days. Maybe months. Everything hinged on staying under the radar.

Ms. Bea ruffled up like a hen with chicks. "Now, see here, little missy, this is your home. I could use some help around this bakery the way you used to do, but there'll be no talk of you paying me a dime."

Tears she'd held back for days curdled in the corners of Sage's eyes. She batted them away. "Thank you."

"Besides, you can't go anywhere until we find those children. I really think we should call Adam."

Sage glanced at her cell phone and then toward the streets again. Time was up.

The kids' safety was the important thing. More important even than Sage's fear of joining her sister in jail.

Out of options, acid burning a hole in her gut, she nodded. "Call him."

With measured movements, Ms. Bea pushed up from the table and started slowly toward the phone. Sage added concern for her foster mom to her growing list of worries.

Vehicle lights swept across the front of the store. A big pickup truck pulled into a parking space.

"Ms. Bea, is that Bowie Trudeau's truck?"

Ms. Bea paused halfway to the counter and turned to look. "Looks like it. What's he doing back? That boy is so thoughtful—he's probably decided to work on my oven tonight while I'm not using it. Bless his heart. He worries about every old lady in town."

The truck door swung open and Bowie's long, jean-clad legs appeared as he stepped onto the street. He reached to the back of the long cab, opened a door and lifted out a small child.

"Paisley!" The chair clattered backward as Sage shot up and started toward the door.

Bowie came striding across the sidewalk toward her, Paisley in his arms. The strangest feeling surged through Sage. An adrenaline rush, she supposed, from seeing Paisley safe and protected in Bowie's care.

Apparently, Bowie Trudeau was still one of the good guys.

Sage pushed the bakery's glass door open and waited as they came inside.

Ryder entered last, head down, dragging his feet. She didn't know whether to scold him or hug him.

She put a hand on the boy's shoulder and, worry in her voice, asked, "Where have you been? You scared me to death. I've been frantic searching for you."

His head dropped lower, along with his bottom lip.

Bowie lowered Paisley to stand on the black-and-white checkerboard tile. "I take it these are your kids?"

His tone was a mixture of concern and accusation. She could see the questions swirling around behind those almost black irises. Goodness, he had pretty eyes. Had she ever noticed them in high school?

"My niece and nephew. Where did you find them?"

"Under the bunk in my workshop."

"What?" She blinked a half dozen times, trying to comprehend. "How? I don't understand."

"That makes two of us. Apparently they decided to hitch a ride in the back of my truck."

Sage's fingers went to her mouth. "I can't believe it.

I mean, I do believe you, but why would they do such a thing?"

Bowie's gaze went from her to Ms. Bea and back to the kids. Then, in a tone that made her feel guilty all over again, he said, "That's exactly what I want to know."

Bowie watched the play of emotion on Sage's face. She'd been scared to pieces when he'd arrived. And when she'd seen the kids, relief and confusion had replaced the fear.

Obviously, she cared, but regardless of her concerned reaction, he wanted to know why kids this young would run away.

Sage went to her haunches in front of the boy, her fashionable jeans stretching tight across shapely, athletic thighs. She used to be a runner, and he recalled watching her long, smooth strides, her black hair flowing out behind her as she'd smoked the competition. Funny that he'd think of that now.

"Ryder, it's dangerous to get into a stranger's vehicle." She flashed a glance at Bowie as if to apologize for calling him a stranger. But he *was* an unknown entity to the kids, and after thirteen years, to her too. "Why did you do that?"

"I wanted to go home. He said he was going to the city."

"Oh." Her pale green eyes lifted to his again. "The kids have been living in Kansas City."

Bowie nodded. "That explains why they picked my truck."

Sage put her hands on Ryder's shoulders and in a tender voice that made his chest ache, said, "Mr. Trudeau is going to a different city, Ryder. Besides, we've discussed this. We can't go home right now."

The boy's face clouded up. He wore a perpetual expression of worry, something an eight-year-old shouldn't have. It bothered Bowie. A lot.

"But what about Mama?"

Sage drew in a breath that said they'd had this conversation, too, and she was helpless to make the little boy understand. "Your mama is—"

"—sick!" The word exploded from Ryder. "She's sick, Aunt Sage. I have to go take care of her."

Sage's long black lashes swept low as she closed her eyes, waited a beat, and tried again. "Someone is looking after your mom. She'll be okay."

The boy didn't appear convinced. A frown puckered between his eyebrows. He pressed his lips in a straight line.

Meanwhile, Paisley, a tiny thing and cute as a kitten, pressed close to her brother and rubbed the corner of the lovey against one cheek. Clearly, Ryder was her anchor, the person she depended on.

Which made Bowie wonder, how long had they been with Sage? Why couldn't they go home? Where was Amy?

Why was he letting any of that bother him?

But he knew why. He cared about kids, especially kids in need. This was why he supported Isaiah House, the New Orleans's shelter.

"I got to go find her, Aunt Sage. Sometimes Mama falls down in weird places and can't get home by herself. I'm supposed to take care of her. She said so."

With those few words, understanding seeped into Bowie's consciousness. He suffered a moment of déjà vu, a hard clutch behind his ribs and a giant dose of empathy for the boy. He remembered feeling exactly the same way about his meth-addicted mother. She'd been his responsibility. He'd thought he had to take care of her. He had tried. That he'd failed still bothered him sometimes.

He hoped he was wrong about Amy, but he probably wasn't.

This was none of his business, but he'd been in Ryder's shoes. If not for an aunt and uncle who'd cared for him the way Sage seemed to care for these kids he would likely still be lost in New Orleans's underbelly.

Going to a crouch beside Sage, he said to the boy, "Remember that promise I made to you and Paisley?"

Ryder looked as if he expected Bowie to renege now that he'd found someone to take the kids off his hands. "You said you'd buy us ice cream."

"A man's only as good as his word." Bowie glanced up at Sage. "If it's okay with your aunt, we'll go right now before The Scoop closes."

One of Sage's magazine-perfect eyebrows arched. "The Scoop?"

She crouched next to him, so close their sides nearly brushed and he caught the faintest hint of a warm perfume. When she'd turned her head to look at him, Bowie could see the dark rim circling her green irises.

He tried not to notice how beautiful she was or how his pulse, the silly thing, got a little erratic from her nearness.

He wasn't a kid anymore. He knew better than to let his emotions get entangled with Sage Walker again. Being abandoned by her once was like the old adage, once burned, twice warned.

Not going to happen.

Keeping a promise to a child was a different matter.

"Ice cream place," he said. "Fairly new. What do you say? Up for a double dip?"

Humor brightened her expression. "I can't be the cause of a man going back on his word. But the kids need to eat something healthy first."

Ryder jerked a thumb toward Bowie. "He fixed us a sandwich."

As if she wasn't accustomed to anyone doing something nice for her, Sage's face softened in wonder. "You did?"

When she looked at him like that, as if fixing a ham

sandwich was right up there with world peace, Bowie felt a little embarrassed. But pleased too.

With a shrug, he pressed his hands to his knees and stood. “Load up.”

To the baker, he said, “Ms. Bea, you want to go for ice cream?”

“No, you kids go on. I’ll close up the bakery and head home. These old bones are weary. Sage, honey, I’ll see you there later? You still remember the way?”

Sage, one hand on Ryder’s shoulder as if she didn’t trust him not to run, nodded. “Of course. Thank you, Ms. Bea. I can’t tell you how much this means right now.”

“Everything is going to be okay, hon,” Ms. Bea said. “The Lord will work all this for your good. And the good of these children. That’s His promise to anyone who walks uprightly before Him. You just wait and see.”

The words of reassurance left Bowie to wonder all the more. What was going on in Sage Walker’s life?

# Chapter Three

Inside the cute little ice cream shop, Sage sat across from Bowie Trudeau amazed by all that had transpired in the last few hours. Not only had Ms. Bea welcomed her with open arms, she'd reconnected with an old friend.

Maybe Ms. Bea was right. Maybe things were going to work out after all.

As long as no one came looking for Ryder and Paisley, they'd all three be fine.

Here in this small, out-of-the-way town, far from Kansas City and Amy's trouble, they had the best chance of avoiding attention.

She glanced at the two young ones huddled together beside her in a corner of the booth licking orange sherbet cones. Paisley snuggled close to her brother as if terrified he'd disappear, and Ryder's anxious protectiveness worried Sage. She didn't know what the kids had experienced before she'd arrived in Kansas City, but she did know it hadn't been good. They desperately needed stability, something they'd never had with their mother. If she could remain in Sundown Valley even for a short while maybe they'd have a chance to heal emotionally.

If anyone asked too many questions, though, she'd have no choice but to load Paisley and Ryder in the car and find another safe place.

Keep moving. That was her mantra. Moving was what she did, what she'd done from the time she'd gone into foster care as a kid, always with the hope that the next placement, the next town, the next situation would be better.

Life had to be better, safer, happier somewhere.

But where?

Lately, moving on had only made matters worse. She was tired of the uncertainty.

Fretting, she stabbed the tip of a plastic spoon into her frozen yogurt and tried to get her mind on something, anything, else.

Her gaze fell on the empty table space in front of Bowie. "You didn't order any ice cream."

He sat across from them, his tall, well-built body taking up a very manly portion of the bench seat. Sitting slightly cantilevered, one of his long legs extended into the walk space.

He patted his flat belly. "Watching my weight."

She laughed. "That used to be my line."

Sun spokes crinkled around his eyes. "I remember."

He did? Had she been that obnoxious about staying thin enough to become the next big supermodel?

Another failure she didn't want to think about.

"Tell me about you, Bowie," she said. "Catch me up."

With all the worries she had pressing, and regardless of her fatigue, these few minutes of respite with an old pal and a cup of chocolate yogurt felt good. They smoothed the edges from her very rough day.

Bowie shifted in the booth, his wide cowboy hands splayed on the tabletop as if holding the thing in place. He had never liked to talk, especially about himself. He was more of a listener.

"Not much to tell. I still work on the family ranch and go to church on Sundays. Bible study on Tuesdays."

Sage rolled her eyes. "I'm sure there's more to the last thirteen years than that. Did I hear Ms. Bea mention a wedding?"

"This afternoon. My cousin Wade married a teacher from Tulsa. Kyra. Great girl. Wade deserved her after his first wife."

"I didn't realize he'd been married before."

"Yeah. She left him. And their triplets."

"Triplets!" A shocked chuckle ripped from her. "I can't imagine wild Wade with three kids."

A tiny curve of lips set Bowie's cleft chin into play next to a sculpted jaw that would need a razor soon, although she thought she'd like the scruffy look on him. She'd always appreciated the chin dimple.

"Wild Wade grew up. He's domesticated now."

She tilted her head, grinning a little at the notion and feeling nostalgic. "What about you, Bowie? Anyone domesticated you yet?"

She was only making conversation, not fishing for information about his love life. Romance was way, way off her agenda.

He leaned back against the maroon booth, his smile still hovering in the most appealing manner. "I've always been domesticated."

He had, as a matter of fact. Quiet, settled, dependable. Her exact opposite. "What about Yates?"

The smile wilted. A shadow crossed his handsome face and knitted a frown between his eyes. "Yates joined the military after Trent got killed."

She placed a hand on the forearm he'd rested on the tabletop. It was rock hard with thick muscle and as warm as the man himself. "Ms. Bea told me about Trent's horrific accident. Trudeaus have seen their share of tragedy. I'm so sorry."

"Yeah." His chest rose and fell in a long breath. "Trent was a good kid."

"You miss him."

"I miss them all."

She knew he spoke of his aunt and uncle who'd died in a plane crash her senior year. Before she'd gone off to seek fame and fortune. Before she'd made a mess of things.

She'd attended the funeral with most of the town, stunned by the loss of so vibrant a couple. The Trudeau boys, as everyone called them, walked around like zombies for weeks, devastated and in shock.

Even then, Bowie had said little, and she realized he'd listened to her woes but had never dumped his heartache on her.

Had she really been that self-focused?

"Where is Yates now?"

Again, that shadow sailed over him, like a cloud over the warm sun. "He doesn't communicate much."

That was likely all the information she'd get about the oldest cousin, the one she'd dated briefly.

But that was a long, long time ago. Lots of muddy water had passed under her proverbial bridge since then.

She took a bite of her Froyo, letting the frozen chocolate melt on her tongue while she contemplated the man across from her. He was the same but different, and she had the most intriguing reaction to this grown-up version of Bowie.

Not attraction exactly, but definitely interest, something she would not allow to grow. Her life was already complicated beyond words. No need to add to her problems. Especially when her stay in Sundown Valley would most likely be short-lived.

But she really wanted him to be her friend again. The Lord knew she needed a trustworthy friend, and those were hard to find in her world. Bowie had always been a person to trust. Was he still?

"What about you?" he asked. "What have you been up to since leaving Sundown Valley? It's been a lot of years."

Avoiding his gaze, she stirred her Froyo. "Obviously, the modeling dream went bust."

"I wondered," he said, his voice soft. "Their loss."

She tilted her head, a sweet ache throbbing somewhere in the region of her heart. "Kind of you to say that."

"Truth, not kindness. You had to be the prettiest girl in New York. If the modeling world didn't see that, they missed out."

Again, his remarks made her ache. If he knew of all her failures, of how she'd sabotaged her own opportunities for success, he wouldn't be so easy on her.

"There are lots of tall, beautiful women in New York." She felt uncomfortable including herself in that group. She was Amazonian tall, running had made her lean and shapely, and people said she was pretty, but she'd learned the hard way that physical attributes could be both a blessing and a curse. "Not every pretty girl is cut out for the modeling industry."

"Tough business?"

He had no idea. She'd been a naive country bumpkin, thinking her looks would open doors. They had. Except she'd walked through the wrong ones.

"Very tough. So, let's talk about something else. What's going on with Ms. Bea? She moves as if she's in pain."

"She is. Some kind of degenerative arthritis, I think. It's gotten worse in the last year."

"That makes my heart hurt."

"Yeah." He rubbed a spot over his chest as though his actually ached. "I wonder how much longer she can run the bakery."

"Is she talking about giving it up?" The notion bothered Sage. A lot. She couldn't imagine Sundown Valley without the Bea Sweet and Ms. Bea.

"Once or twice," he said, "but it would crush her to see it go. That bakery is her life."

Sage nodded, leaning in a little, close enough to catch his scent, a mix of fresh autumn air and new leather. "Did you know her family has owned and operated that same store since statehood?"

"Doesn't surprise me." His lips twitched. "Some of the bakery's equipment must have come over on the *May-flower*."

"And you're nice enough to work on it for her."

"She's a good lady. I don't mind." Bowie hitched his chin toward the kids. "Someone's fading fast."

Sure enough, Paisley's head dipped low, almost on her chest, her half-eaten sherbet cone now lying sideways on the tabletop.

Before she could rescue the cone, Bowie grabbed a napkin and scooped it up. Without a word, he went to the counter and returned with the sherbet safely tucked inside a lidded cup.

"She might want this tomorrow." He handed Sage the cup.

She added *thoughtful* to Bowie's nice guy qualities.

"I guess we should go." Truth was, she was reluctant to leave. She'd become reenergized during the few minutes in the ice cream shop. Must be a sugar rush from the Froyo.

But the kids were exhausted. Even Ryder had begun to wilt, his eyes droopy.

Sage turned to lift the sleeping girl, but Bowie put a hand on her arm. "I'll get her."

With a grateful nod, she scooted out of the booth with Ryder and the leftover ice cream, and once more enjoyed a warm tingle at seeing the little girl cradled in Bowie's strong rancher's arms.

"I'll follow you in my truck to Ms. Bea's house."

"No need for that."

"Sure there is." He gazed down at the sleeping child. "Somebody's got to carry the princess."

"She's tiny. I can lift her."

"Nope. It says right there on my man card. A real man carries all sleeping princesses."

She laughed, appreciating Bowie's gentle humor. Truth was, she appreciated a lot of things about Bowie Trudeau and offered a quick prayer of thanks that this kindhearted friend was one of the first people she'd encountered in Sundown Valley.

Ice cream, conversation and a good man.

If only life was always this simple.

Bowie followed Sage's Jeep to Ms. Bea's house. Though it was the neighborly thing to do, he probably shouldn't have. He should have helped her get the kids in her vehicle and said his goodbyes at the now-closed bakery.

Back in high school, he'd always had this awful compunction to follow Sage Walker around like a guard dog. Or a puppy. But high school was eons ago and he was no longer inclined to sticky relationships. Yet, here he was outside Ms. Bea's house, parked behind Sage's white Jeep.

Wade would call him a sucker and then feel sorry for him, one of the reasons he'd never told a soul about his feelings for the dark, willowy beauty whose laugh could keep him going for days and whose tears could turn him wrong side out.

Unrequited love was a real pain.

He'd dealt with that unpleasantness the day she'd left Sundown Valley.

Now that she was back, he'd show her kindness, as he did everyone, as his faith commanded, but kindness was as far as he could go.

He hopped out of the truck and, with his long-legged strides, was at the back door of her Jeep before she was.

In this older residential section of town, streetlights were sporadic, half of them no longer working. It didn't matter in Sundown Valley. Streets were generally safe, even if they were darker than sin.

Across the street, a pair of dogs barked at the strangers. A porch light came on and a man peered out, then yelled for the dogs to hush.

Bowie carefully removed Paisley from her car seat and held her diagonally across his shoulder. She was small, weighing little, and as she snuggled into the side of his neck, tenderness settled over him. She stirred, clutching the lovey in one tiny hand. Not wanting to drop the treasured blanket, Bowie tucked it in around her.

Sage walked alongside him, guiding a wobbly Ryder up the single step onto Ms. Bea's wooden porch.

"Is that the same old porch swing?" she mused, her tone nostalgic.

"As far as I know."

"We solved the world's problems in that swing."

Apparently, not all of them.

The door opened and the porch light flared as Bea pushed aside the old-fashioned storm door to let them inside. The Cunningham place was older and had never been fancy, but its two stories and many rooms were homey and cozy, a place where lots of children had found love and renewed hope.

If he was guessing, he'd say this was exactly what these children needed right now.

Ms. Bea led the way, shuffling along in a pink belted bathrobe and brown slippers, down a hall to the back bedrooms.

"The stairs are getting to be too much for me, so I'll put you three back here for tonight. Sage, if you're up to it, hon, you can air some of the upstairs rooms tomorrow and let the kids each pick one."

"This is fine for now, Ms. Bea." Sage guided Ryder inside a small bedroom to a set of bunk beds. “Don’t fuss over us.”

Ryder cast a nervous glance toward Bowie. “Put my sister on the bottom bed. She might roll off and get hurt if she’s up high.”

The boy, who appeared tired enough to drop, turned back the covers on the bottom bunk and waited while Bowie placed the little girl on the bed. Sage removed her shoes and socks.

“Don’t bother to undress her, Sage,” Ms. Bea said. “She’s tuckered. Her clothes won’t hurt these bed linens.”

With a nod, Sage reached for the covers, but Ryder was already there. He covered his sister and whispered something in her ear. Paisley’s eyes opened, she stared at the adults and then at her brother before snuggling down with her lovey and going back to sleep.

Satisfied, the fierce little protector toed off his worn athletic shoes and, in floppy socks, climbed onto the top bunk.

Apparently, sleeping in his clothes was not an unusual occurrence.

Sage stood beside the bunks, her height giving her easy access to the boy. “Everything will be okay. You get some sleep and tomorrow we’ll do something fun.”

Ryder didn’t look as if he believed her. And those eyes of doubt burned inside Bowie like a stoked furnace. The kid didn’t trust anyone, not even his aunt.

Again, he wondered why. What had happened to this boy? And why didn’t he trust his own aunt?

As the adults started to leave the room, Sage reached for the light switch.

Ryder bolted upright. “Don’t!” Eyes wide and anxious, he pled, “Leave the light on. Okay? Paisley gets scared in the dark.”

With a sorrowful tug in his gut, Bowie figured Paisley wasn't the only one.

Leaving the light on and the door opened a crack, the adults stepped into the hallway.

"Sage, you're across the hall in case they need you," Ms. Bea said. "Lock up when Bowie leaves. I'm heading to bed. Four o'clock comes early." She patted Bowie on the upper arm. "Good night."

Bowie watched with concern as the older woman disappeared toward the front of the house. Then he followed Sage back into the living room.

"I forgot that she has to get up that early," Bowie said.

"Me, too, but people want their doughnuts hot and fresh and early. She has to mix the dough, get it to rise and make the pastries all before the bakery opens at six."

"Don't forget the coffee."

"When I lived here as a teenager, I remember the smell of coffee wafting up the stairs to my bedroom in the wee hours while it was still dark. Mr. Ron would head for the bakery to get things started while Ms. Bea got us kids up and off to school. Sometimes there'd be seven or eight of us. She always made sure we had a hearty breakfast before she left for work."

"Now that Ron's gone, she carries the entire load at the bakery."

"I wonder why she hasn't hired someone?" Sage rubbed the back of her neck as if she'd driven a long way today and was as tired as the kids.

"Jan Templeton comes in part-time. Mostly counter help. No bakers."

"No one wants to get up at four, I guess, to make dough. If it wasn't for Ryder and Paisley, I'd..."

She let the words trail and Bowie was right back to wondering what she was doing here. And for how long. Neither of which was any of his business.

"You'd what?" Yes, he was stupid that way.

Sage shook her head and pushed the storm door open with the flat of her hand. Apparently, she was trying to get rid of him.

Right. Good. He still had work to do at home.

Time to move on. "You're tired. I'll go."

The chains on the swing squeaked as Sage sat down and patted the wooden slats next to her. "Sit a minute. Please. I'm too wound up to sleep yet. The back of my neck feels like it could crack."

He really should go. Sitting close to Sage might stir up all kinds of things better left buried.

"Tense from driving?" Gripping the chain with one hand, he steadied the swing and settled next to her.

He was terrible at following his own advice. To make matters worse, he was sorely tempted to use his big, strong rancher's hands to massage Sage's tight shoulders.

Years ago, he would have, but they didn't know each other that well anymore.

Hard-won wisdom said to keep his hands to himself.

Sage stretched one long leg out in front of her, the other curled beneath her to set the swing into gentle motion.

The night air was cool but pleasant, the small town noisier than the country, but still tranquil.

A car puttered past, lights sweeping in a white arc along the street, and then, except for the squeak and creak of the slow-moving swing, silence returned to the dark porch.

Bowie could bear the mystery no longer. "What brings you back to Sundown Valley, Sage?"

Sage inhaled and let the breath out slower than necessary. "Ryder and Paisley. And Ms. Bea, of course. We needed a place to stay for a while."

For a while. A telling phrase. She was here, but not to stay.

Bowie wondered if she was still as restless as she'd

been in high school, the girl who'd never lived anywhere long, thanks to foster care and her propensity to run away when things got rough.

Then he wondered why he cared.

"Am I prying too much if I ask what's going on?"

"Yes, but I'll tell you anyway." She shifted on the slats, bringing one knee up on the swing as if placing a border between them. "Amy's in trouble, and the kids needed me."

The statement opened up a dozen other questions. "What kind of trouble?"

Sage was silent for a long moment as if gathering her strength. When she finally spoke, she sounded tired and sad. "She's a meth addict, Bowie."

"I suspected as much." He heard the harshness in his voice, a harshness that caused Sage to halt the swing and stare at him.

"You did? How?"

Bowie swallowed the bitter taste rising in his throat like a stomach virus. "Something Ryder said about taking care of his mother when she fell down in strange places."

"That rips my heart out."

"Mine too." His fist involuntarily closed on the cold chain, pressing the links deep into his flesh. "Addicts not only hurt themselves, they hurt the people who love them most. And that's wrong."

He tried to keep his resentment toward his mother hidden, tried to forget what she'd done to him. Sometimes, like today when he'd seen himself in an eight-year-old's eyes, his own troubled history raised its ugly head.

As much as he resisted thoughts of his mother, he wondered what had happened to her, wondered if she was okay. Who helped her up when she fell asleep in weird places?

Questions he tried to turn over to God, but they rose again and again to haunt him. Sometimes he felt as if he'd abandoned her instead of the other way around. Twisted, but true.

Sage's warm hand touched his tightened biceps. "Sorry. I didn't mean to upset you."

He'd told her a little about his life before he'd come to live with his aunt and uncle. Not everything, of course, but enough for her to know he'd lived the first ten years of his life on the streets.

"You didn't. Drug addicts do." Jaw tight, the hurt and anger he usually kept stifled, boiled up. "I can abide anything and anyone but a druggie. They deserve what they get."

Sage went as silent as a midnight snowfall. Her knee flexed and she set the swing in motion again.

Bowie forced his fingers to relax against the chain. "My turn to apologize. Amy's your sister. I shouldn't have said that."

"It's okay. You have a right to feel that way."

"The Lord would probably argue about that, but regardless, I shouldn't dump my harsh feelings on you. You're the innocent party in this case, the rescuer."

She went quiet again as she dropped her foot to the wooden porch and stared at the trellis of pink roses clinging to the last bits of summer.

He'd hurt her feelings about her sister, whether she admitted it or not. He wished he'd said nothing at all the way he usually did. Sage, even after all this time, had a way of making him talk about things better left inside.

He eased away from the painful subject. "I wonder how many kids have sat on this swing and talked."

"Or made out."

Bowie heard the smile in her voice.

"Provocative." He chuckled, letting the tension from before ease out with the soothing back and forth motion of the swing. "You said that to make me laugh, didn't you?"

He turned his face toward her. Man, she was gorgeous. Even in the shadowy moonlight, she looked more regal and beautiful than an ancient Egyptian queen.

*Looks aren't everything, Trudeau. Remember that.*

"Yes. I did." She bumped his shoulder with hers, and, for a fraction of a second, the years faded. He recalled the awkward teenager, in love with the girl who thought of him only as a friend.

He didn't need to go through that again.

Many was the time he'd sat beside her on this swing, wanting to kiss her, and he wondered what would have happened if he had. If he'd crossed over that friendship line and let her know how he felt. Would they have become a couple? Would she have stayed in Sundown Valley?

He'd never been willing to take the chance.

Still wasn't.

His best advice to himself was to let sleeping dogs lie.

# *Chapter Four*

Sage was absolutely sure she heard a rooster crow. She sat up on the pullout couch in Ms. Bea's home office and stretched, letting yesterday flood through her mind as she listened again for the unexpected rooster crow.

When none came, she pushed back the comforter and tiptoed across the hall for a peek at the kids. Ryder and Paisley still slept, their faces bathed in the innocence of resting childhood, free from the worries that plagued them when awake. Even the perpetual frown was erased from Ryder's forehead.

Sage leaned a forearm and her head against the door frame and whispered a prayer. They desperately needed a change for the better. So far, she'd come up short in the healthy lifestyle department herself. How could she expect to make a difference for Ryder and Paisley?

"By your grace and direction, Lord," she whispered. "I don't know what else to do."

A new Christian, she was still finding her way. Most of her prayers were more hope than faith. She wondered if they counted or if God ignored them, waiting for better.

Letting the children sleep on, she hit the downstairs shower and then dressed in a rumpled pair of jeans and a long-sleeved T-shirt she'd stuffed into a duffel bag yesterday morning. Sometime today, she'd air those upstairs rooms, do some laundry and shake the wrinkles out of their getaway clothes. First, she'd repay Ms. Bea by volunteering at the bakery.

Right now, she longed for a good jolt of caffeine. If she'd hoped for the smell of freshly brewed coffee, she was out of luck. The house was chilly with only the scent of Sage's own shampoo dancing around her. Ms. Bea was already gone for the day, though it was only seven. The morning coffee routine was likely buried with her husband.

In the homey old-fashioned kitchen with ruffled red curtains over the sink, sunlight shafted across the brick-patterned linoleum and highlighted the wear and tear from years of foster children.

There was something about the sameness in this house that Sage found comforting.

Spotting the coffee maker and a can of coffee waiting on the counter next to a clear sugar bowl, a mug and a spoon, Sage smiled.

How had Bea remembered after all these years?

She set the coffee maker to brew, leaning on the counter to wait, toe tapping, her brain whirling, searching like a worn-out hard drive unable to find a file.

That had become her life. Going from one place to another searching for something she could never find.

Now two children were riding that same lonely train. Somehow, someway, she had to get them off. She had to give them a stable life, security. She had to rebuild their trust in caring adults, in life itself.

The question was, how?

She'd just poured a steaming cup when Ryder stumbled into the kitchen, scratching at a head that looked more like a porcupine than a boy and looking bewildered.

"Where is this place?"

"A good friend's house. Is Paisley awake?"

"Not yet. I'm hungry."

"Then get showered and dressed and we'll go into town and find something." No way was she digging in Ms. Bea's pantry without permission. That would be taking the friendship a little too far. "I want to talk to Ms. Bea and maybe help her this morning."

"The lady at the bakery?" Ryder asked.

"Yes. Ms. Bea. She owns the bakery and this house. We need to help her out since she's letting us stay here for a little while."

How long? How long before she had to run again? And what was she to do about the kids' schooling?

She didn't dare try to enroll them here in Sundown Valley.

At the word *bakery*, Ryder's countenance brightened. "Can I have doughnuts for breakfast? Chocolate with sprinkles?"

"Maybe for dessert."

He sighed, his bottom lip poking out in a way she was quickly coming to recognize as argumentative. "Mom let me eat whatever I wanted."

Sage moved right past the comment. Amy wasn't sober enough to feed them half the time. Ryder was the caregiver who rustled up whatever he could find for Paisley and himself.

"The shower is down the hall next to the bedroom you slept in. I'll get your clean clothes from the car. If you don't argue, we'll negotiate that doughnut after breakfast."

Ryder, scratching at his chest, trudged out of the kitchen and did as she asked.

After bringing in their meager bags and a basketful of dirty laundry she'd scraped from the floor of Amy's ratty apartment, Sage helped Paisley bathe and dress for the day, plaiting her sandy hair in a long French braid that matched her own. The look pleased the silent child. Sage knew this because Paisley, perched on her knees atop the vanity, turned her head side to side, staring at her image in the bathroom mirror with a smile.

Sage kissed the top of her niece's shampoo-scented

head, wondering why she chose not to speak. She could talk. That wasn't the issue. She talked to Ryder, but she only shook her head in answer to any questions from adults.

It worried her, this fear, this lack of trust, but it did not surprise her.

Getting ready took longer with kids than she'd expected, and when Ryder pounded on the bathroom door declaring that he'd heard a chicken, he wouldn't rest until they'd investigated the phenomenon.

Sure enough three speckled hens and a cocky rooster strutted around an enclosure in Ms. Bea's backyard, pecking at what appeared to be corn sprinkled on the grass.

"This is new," she mumbled. She hadn't dreamed the rooster crow after all.

"Can we pet them?"

"I don't know." Sage knew less about chickens than she did kids. Which wasn't much. "We'll ask Ms. Bea when we get to the bakery."

The little girl leaned close to her brother's ear. Sage heard nothing but Ryder nodded.

"Paisley's hungry. We should go now."

Sage herded them toward the Jeep. If she was going to help out at the bakery, she had to get up earlier. But dragging the kids out at four or five in the morning was a problem. A problem to worry about later, after she talked to Ms. Bea, after she decided if she could stay in Sundown Valley more than a day or two.

By the time they arrived at the Bea Sweet, the morning rush had slackened. Ms. Bea still bustled about, serving, cleaning, ringing up purchases.

"There you are." She smiled at the children as she circled a disinfectant cloth over one of the square tables. "Did you sleep okay? I guess you're hungry, huh? Or did Sage rustle up some breakfast at the house?"

"I didn't want to impose. We'll buy our breakfast."

Bea's fleshy face registered disapproval. "Impose? What kind of talk is that? You lived in that house. You're one of my kids. Whatever I have is yours to use."

A sudden, unexpected surge of emotion caught Sage off guard. She'd done nothing to earn Bea's trust or kindness, and yet there it was.

While she grappled to hold back tears—definitely not her style—the tiny bell over the entrance jingled and a graying gentleman in a business suit entered.

A welcome distraction.

"Good morning, Danny." Ms. Bea shuffled slowly toward the register. "Keeping banker's hours again?"

The man chuckled. "As always, Bea, as always. Is my order ready?"

"Give me a jiff and I'll box it up fresh. I need to check the oven right quick first."

Sage placed a hand on the older woman's arm. "I can box the order."

Bea's look of grateful relief, on top of her kindness about the house, started Sage's emotions bubbling again.

Goodness. Must be exhaustion. She should have stayed in bed a while longer for this one morning.

"I'd appreciate it, honey. The First Bank has a standing order for a dozen mixed doughnuts. Do you remember how to do that?"

"If I don't, I can ask."

She guided the children to a table with the promise of an egg biscuit and apple juice and then, hoping Ryder would see fit to stay put, rounded the counter.

After another thorough hand wash, she found the to-go boxes with the see-through tops, donned serving gloves and counted out the baker's dozen of sprinkles, chocolate, maple and glazed, her mouth watering at the fresh, warm pastries.

When was the last time she'd had an actual meal? Yesterday's ice cream and bear claw didn't exactly qualify and she'd been so upset the previous days trying to figure out how to keep Amy out of jail and what to do about the children, she didn't remember eating much of anything. During the long drive to Oklahoma, she'd fed the kids at fast-food places, but figured she should reserve the remainder of her meager funds in case they had to keep traveling.

It reminded her of those early days of starving herself to fit the ultrathin supermodel image. For all the good it had done.

In minutes she handed over the filled pastry box while Ms. Bea manned the cash register. She refused to take offense that her former foster mother didn't ask her to handle the money. Bea didn't know her anymore. Not really.

But she had opened her heart and her home and that was more than Sage had expected or deserved.

After the banker departed, Bea showed Sage around the bakery and mentioned some tasks she'd gladly relinquish. The kitchen, Sage noted, still bore the remnants of this morning's preparations. Flour on the butcher's block prep table and the concrete floor, pans and bowls waiting in the industrial stainless steel sinks to be washed and put away.

"I'll clean up, Ms. Bea, if you want me to while you handle the counter and the register."

"Sounds good, but you feed those babies first. This can wait."

"Egg biscuit and juice okay?"

"Anything you want, honey. And if you work for me, you get paid. I can only offer minimum but it comes with room and board."

"Ms. Bea—" Sage started.

The baker waved her off with a pointed index finger. "Get those little ones fed and hush your arguing. You're still too good at that."

She softened the reminder of Sage's recalcitrant attitude with a smile. When she and Amy had first come to live with Bea and Ron, she'd been angry and rebellious. The couple's consistent correction, unflinching love and steadfast faith had settled her enough to finish high school.

Bea and Ron were the only anchors she'd ever had.

Feeling more hopeful than she had in weeks, maybe months, Sage put the other worries out of her mind for a minute while she ushered the kids to the little bistro table in the kitchen and set out their breakfast before turning her attention to the cleanup chores.

Occasionally, she'd hear the entrance bell jingle and the pleasant hum of conversation. The residents of Sundown Valley had always liked Bea and Ron Cunningham, and the bakery was a morning hub of coffee drinkers at the tables and business people grabbing food and drink to-go. Lingering for a chat and an update on town news was expected. She supposed that hadn't changed with Ron's death.

What *had* changed, she noticed now as she hadn't last night, was the number and variety of baked goods Ms. Bea offered. The display case choices were limited and the chalkboard menu was only half filled.

"You don't bake cakes and pies anymore?" she asked when Bea limped into the kitchen with an empty doughnut tray.

"After Ron passed, I had to cut back. Now, I only bake bread once a week, pies never and cakes rarely."

Sage smiled. "But a wedding cake for Wade Trudeau?"

"Heather Trudeau was one of my best friends. The least I can do is bake a cake for her boys. They're the only ones I do that for. Usually," she said with a grin that let Sage know she was still a soft touch. "Folks seem to prefer the pastries and quick sandwich fare anyway."

In other words, Bea couldn't keep up with daily baking by herself.

"Bowie mentioned a local woman who helps out occasionally."

"Jan Templeton. Remember her? Tanya Templeton's mother."

"Right. I remember Tanya." Tanya was one of her least favorite memories from high school.

"Jan only comes in on Saturday mornings. I close at noon, but the early rush is just as hectic as ever. Why, every armchair quarterback in Sundown gathers around those tables to hash out the Friday night games, and the other half of the town wants Bea's sweets for a weekend breakfast treat."

"Have you considered closing at noon every day?" She didn't state the obvious. Bea couldn't go on working like this forever. Her arthritis seemed every bit as bad this morning as it had last night after she'd been on her feet all day. She was hurting, barely getting around.

"No. No. The kids come in after school for their snacks." Bea shook her whitening blond head. "I'd miss them too much. The way this town has blessed me, I can't let them down like that. They need this bakery."

Sage knew she'd said enough. She was a visitor, not family and not someone close enough to offer advice.

Ryder appeared at her side. "Can I have a doughnut now?"

Just then, the doorbell tinkled.

"I'll go." Ms. Bea dried her hands on a towel and slowly followed Ryder to the display case.

Listening to the friendly exchange of conversation in the outer area, Sage finished wiping down the prep table and took up the broom.

Ryder, with Paisley clinging to him, her lovey and a

sprinkled doughnut, came back to the bistro table to eat his treat.

"How about a glass of milk with that?"

Ryder exchanged looks with his sister before nodding. "Paisley too. But not a lot. She'll waste it."

Ms. Bea probably still fed leftover scraps to the alley cats out back, but the kids would discover them soon enough.

When the bell jingled again, signifying the customer had left, Bea stuck her head around the doorway into the kitchen. "Will you check the proofing box? I'm running short on Long Johns."

"Some things never change." Sage grinned as she went to the device and peered at the dough through the tempered glass.

"It looks ready, Ms. Bea. Nice and fluffy."

The baker shuffled back to the kitchen, a hand to one hip. "Honey, do you mind handling the front while I work this dough? My old hip is hollering a little bit today."

"Sure." She washed her hands for what had to be the tenth time. "Bowie said you've considered selling out since the arthritis has gotten so bad."

Bea's expression was so sad, Sage wished she'd kept her mouth shut.

"I know it's inevitable, hon, but the idea is more painful than burning a hand on the doughnut fryer. And let me tell you, I've done that a time or three."

"I remember how upset Mr. Ron would get when you burned yourself."

"He took such good care of me. Always trying to carry his load and mine too."

"He loved you a lot."

"Finest man I ever knew." Bea fisted a hand over her flour-dusted left chest. "He'd be brokenhearted if he knew

I was considering selling this bakery. He loved it almost as much as he loved me."

"I think he'd understand."

"Sure he would. Bless his soul. But the idea of leaving Sundown Valley without a bakery wouldn't sit well with him. Or me either. The only ones who've offered so far want my building but not the bakery business."

"That's sad."

"So I keep on baking and plan to as long as I can. Maybe some eager young baker will come along and want the business, someone who loves the smell and feel of yeast dough and the joy of serving friends and neighbors the way I do. It's my ministry, you know." She shrugged. "I'm praying about it. I know the good Lord has a plan for me."

Sage wished she knew the Lord's plan for her and these kids. Right now, the future didn't look too promising.

"I can help out temporarily, Ms. Bea, while we're here."

"How long will that be, honey?"

Sage hung the towel above the sink and, afraid Bea would see the ugly truth in her face, averted her gaze. "I don't know, but not long enough to learn the bakery business."

"Oh, Sage, I hope you didn't think I was hinting for you to buy the business." A small chuckle escaped Bea. "But I wouldn't mind it one bit if you did. I could teach you everything you need to know. You already know quite a bit from working here in high school."

"I'm no baker, Ms. Bea." Not that she objected to the tasks Ms. Bea asked her to do. She didn't. But life was never stable in her world.

Besides, she didn't have an extra penny to spare. She could barely buy gas for her Jeep and food for the kids. A business was out of the question, even if she wanted it, which she didn't. Couldn't.

If Ms. Bea knew the whole story behind her visit, she wouldn't trust her anyway.

She cast a quick glance at the children. Nothing had ever been stable for them. Ever.

They were dandelion puffs blowing in the hot winds of their mother's addiction.

Paisley's doughnut lay half-eaten on a napkin but Ryder's had disappeared. The little girl pushed her leftovers toward him. With a generosity that tweaked a spot behind Sage's ribcage, Ryder folded the partial doughnut into the napkin and pushed it back to his sister.

Bea must have seen the action too because she said, "Ryder, I have plenty of doughnuts. Do you want another?"

His eager nod brought a chuckle to the baker. "I like it when someone appreciates my food."

"I'll get it, Ms. Bea. You need to sit and rest a little bit."

"I do at that." With a sigh, she settled in the chair Ryder had vacated. "Get that child anything he wants. We'll talk about the sugar and his teeth later."

Sugar and teeth were the least of Sage's worries.

# *Chapter Five*

In the office of the main house on Sundown Ranch, Bowie went through yesterday's regular mail, sorting out the bills to pay while leaving the stock contracts for Wade to complete when he returned from his honeymoon. Bowie could handle them if he had to, but Wade was better at the legal stuff.

Swiveling the desktop computer monitor, he logged on to the ranch email before opening his personal account.

He scrolled through, read a couple of subscribed devotionals, a few emails from friends, ever hopeful of hearing from Yates.

As usual, there was nothing. He typed in the last email address he had for his cousin and sent him a few lines. Having little to say, he mentioned Sage's return. He didn't know why except she and Yates had been friends too. They'd even dated for a while, another reason he'd never crossed the threshold from friends to more.

Considering all that happened in the end, he was relieved he hadn't.

A new message posted. Isaiah House, the shelter in New Orleans. The director, Ian Carpenter, sent a regular newsletter update to donors.

Frowning, he read enough to know the shelter, as always, was running on fumes. Ian put every dime back into caring for street people. Sometimes the old brick building needed more work than the coffers could afford.

This time, the plea for donations mentioned the need for new plumbing to meet city code.

Clicking the blue button, he went to PayPal and sent a donation.

Leaning back, he logged off, pleased he could do something but never satisfied that the money was enough.

While he pondered the ministry's plumbing issue, the ranch landline jangled. He glanced at the caller ID. Was this the call he'd been waiting for? The call his friend had told him about last night?

"Sundown Ranch, Bowie speaking."

"Bowie Trudeau, the leather artist?"

Leather artist. He sometimes thought of himself as an artist instead of a hobbyist, but hearing someone else use the term excited every nerve ending. "Yes, ma'am. May I ask who's calling?"

The woman on the other end identified herself as Katherine Pembroke with PJ Enterprises, a major supplier to high-end retailers across the country.

"You name the best store you know, we supply it," she said, with obvious pride. "My team buys only the best and we're always on the lookout for quality custom work by new artists. We're very interested in what you do."

"I'm flattered."

"Don't be. We're particular. Lately, we've made the decision to buy more of our products from local cottage artisans. However, we expect top-notch work. From what I've seen, you do that."

Bowie didn't know what to say except, "Thank you."

"So here is the deal, Mr. Trudeau, I'd like to offer you an opportunity to work for us. To share your gift with a major audience willing to pay premium prices for custom designs and absolutely flawless one-of-a-kind leatherwork. Are you interested?"

"Yes." He'd hear her out, but he tried not to get his hopes up.

"Your designs are unique. I've never seen any quite like

them. And the leather tooling is exquisite. The problem is, three pieces is not enough to take before my board."

"Okay. I'm still unclear about what you want from me."

"More product. I require at least ten to fifteen new designs to convince my board to take you on as one of our full-time suppliers of custom leatherworks."

Ten to fifteen. Not a huge number but he'd need time to get them right, and from her strong, take-charge manner, he knew she'd demand perfection.

"Any specific product you have in mind?"

"At this point, handbags mostly, but other items are welcome to give us a taste of all you can do. Modern designs, not particularly Western, though we want one or two of those too."

Bowie's mind was spinning. He stared at the opposite office wall where a photo hung of the whole Trudeau family, before the tragedies. His aunt and uncle and all four boys, including him.

Heather seemed to smile at him, urging him to follow his dreams. She'd been the first to tell him he had a gift.

"When would you need them?"

"The board meeting is December 21 before we break for the holidays. I'd want them in my hands a day or two beforehand to determine if they meet our standards. If they do, I'll take them in and let the board decide."

A little more than two months. He'd never worked that fast before.

"As much as I'd like to say yes, I don't rush. That's a lot of custom product in a short time."

Fact of the matter, the leatherwork never went as fast as he'd have liked. He had too many other things on his plate to indulge in a hobby.

But this woman wasn't talking about a sometimes hobby. This would be a dream come true, one he'd barely let himself imagine was possible.

Ms. Pembroke's laugh was soft. "You stand to make

a lot of money on that product." She named a price that made his eyes widen.

"I'll send you a contract for ten original custom pieces to take to my board. If they approve and want more, as I believe they will, the price goes up."

Did rich people really pay that kind of money for a purse?

He scrubbed the top of his head with his fingertips.

From those ten pieces alone, he could replace most of the plumbing at Isaiah House. Not all, but a healthy start.

"Send me the contract. I'll have my lawyer take a look."

They completed the call with all the particulars. Then Bowie remained behind the desk for long moments, filtering through their conversation. He wondered if the call was a hoax. Or a scam.

But what would have been the point?

He did a quick online search for PJ Enterprises and discovered they were not only legit, they were exactly what Katherine Pembroke claimed. High-end. Well-connected.

A big deal.

Bowie blew out a breath. His heart pounded.

He gazed at the leather watchband on his wrist. He'd spent hours and hours perfecting this design depicting the sunset over the ranch. Wade wore an identical one. Did Yates still wear his?

His email pinged. PJ Enterprises had already sent him a message with an attached contract.

The woman didn't let any grass grow under her feet.

After a quick response, he downed the last of his now-cold coffee and called his attorney. In what seemed like a whirlwind, the contract was forwarded, the attorney had called back and he'd scrawled his name on the bottom line and returned it to PJ Enterprises.

Ten original designs in two months. More than one a week, though he had a couple of pieces already in progress that might work. Still, a full design and completion per week?

His excited heart battered his ribcage. Excited and more than a little nervous. He who rarely let anything shake him wondered if he'd just made a huge mistake.

Maybe he should have prayed before signing that contract. And talked things over with Wade.

"A commitment is a commitment, cowboy." And, he still had this ranch to run.

Though ranch life was easing toward the slower time of winter, he was still busier than a mouse in a cheese factory.

They'd planted winter wheat on a hundred acres and put up hundreds of hay bales, both horse and cow hay. Cows were worked, culled, and many sent to the market with the remainder to winter over for the calf crop next year.

The Sundown Ranch was in good shape. Had to be or Wade would never have left for a week, even if it was his honeymoon.

Nonetheless, plenty of ranch work remained. Bulls to test and rotate. Cows to preg test. Friends who'd inevitably call on him, especially the widows. Caring for widows was a scriptural command he considered his special brand of living the gospel.

Somehow he'd squeeze in the leatherwork.

He'd awakened early this morning and now he was glad he had. Sleep had been impossible anyway, with his mind on Sage and her niece and nephew. They troubled him, those two little ones. Sage, too, if he was honest. Why had she really come back here after thirteen years away? Surely, during all that time, she'd made closer contacts than Ms. Bea and Sundown Valley. Hadn't she?

To add to his questions about Sage and the kids, his mind swirled around the amazing contract he'd signed.

Trying to calm the jumble of thoughts, he left the office.

He'd barely made it to the living room when three rambunctious toddlers tackled him.

With a laugh, he went down on the patterned living room rug for a little play time.

Mrs. Roberta, the grandmotherly nanny who'd followed the triplets into the room, smiled at the pile of man and babies. "They're glad to see Uncle Bowie."

He wasn't exactly their uncle, though he doted on them like one.

"They doing okay?" He poked his head around Abby who'd decided his chest was a trampoline. "Any issues?"

"All is well. They're busy as beavers and twice as messy, but well and happy."

"Happiest bunch of monkeys I ever saw." He made a roaring sound, like a lion, and pretended to nip at Ben. All three babies chortled in delight and dove at him.

As he wrestled and played, he considered how secure these three were, thanks to Wade's consistent devotion and to Kyra, the new mother under whose attention and love they'd all three bloomed. Healthy, happy, secure.

He couldn't say the same for Ryder and Paisley. They were anxious, watchful and heartrendingly insecure, even with their Aunt Sage.

Worrisome. But not his business.

Except maybe it was. They had hitched a ride in his truck and hidden in his workshop. God commanded a Christian to look after the needy.

He wondered how they were today. How Sage was.

He had to go into town later anyway, needed to look at Ms. Bea's oven. Paying a friendly call on the newcomers was just a neighborly thing to do.

"A man telephoned for you last night. Did you see the note on the fridge?"

Untangling himself from the triplets, Bowie stood. Abby decided to hitch a ride on his boot so he carried her to the kitchen.

Sure enough, a note in Mrs. Roberta's flowing cursive hung from a cow-headed stockyards magnet.

As he read the words, he grinned.

*Come by tomorrow. I might have pie.*

Mrs. Roberta sidled up beside him, smelling of coffee and bacon. Even though she didn't have to, she cooked for the Trudeaus and Riley, their main ranch hand. Bowie had enjoyed a hearty breakfast a while ago.

"If it hadn't been a man's voice on the phone, I would think some lady is wooing you with her cooking skills."

"Not hardly." Amused, Bowie shook his head and headed to the door. "Call me if anything comes up."

"Will do." Absently, she wiggled her fingers at him, already busy refereeing a tug-of-war between Abby and Ben over a toy guitar which twanged in the melee.

He wanted to head to his workshop and spend the day considering new designs, but friends came first. He could brainstorm images while he drove.

After a stop at barn 2 to check on a horse with a cut leg, Bowie drove deeper into the woods and higher up the mountain. The Kiamichi were low, accessible mountains but still windy, remote and sparsely populated. Often the side roads dwindled into nothing but trails accessible by foot, horse or ATV. Such was the road leading to Jinx Vanderbilt's cabin, a barely standing jumble of boards and rocks. At the bottom of a hill, Bowie parked his truck next to Jinx's four-wheel drive and hiked in the last thousand yards.

Jinx met him at the door, peering through an old screen badly in need of repair.

Somewhere in his sixties, Jinx was a wiry fellow, not too tall or too heavy, but with enough muscle to chop wood and stoke his Ashley wood heater. He wore a long gray beard which he claimed covered a scar, though Bowie had never seen it. His hair and eyebrows remained strikingly brown and his gaze was true and honest. Though he dressed in overalls and a T-shirt today, his military jacket was still a comfortable fit.

Bowie pointed at the door. "I can fix that screen for you."

"Oh, never mind that. We got warm pie and hot coffee." He shoved the door open.

Jinx lived a hermit's life and seldom showed his face in town. Most people probably didn't even know he existed. An army vet, he'd come home from war years ago in good shape, only to discover his wife and baby both had died in a hit-and-run a week before. The perpetrator had never been found.

Shattered, Jinx had sold everything he had, bought this run-down hunter's hideaway and left the world behind.

Bowie had made his acquaintance as a kid when his cousins had come up here with some friends to hassle the older man, a story Wade and Yates deeply regretted and were glad Bowie had never told their parents.

Since that occasion, he paid the man regular visits, figuring he owed every veteran in America his respect. In the process, he'd made an interesting friend.

"Pie sounds good." Ducking his head, he stepped over the threshold and entered the dim confines.

Jinx's tiny living space consisted of a wooden rocker, a fairly new leather couch Bowie had hauled up the mountain himself, a small television perched atop a dresser, rabbit ear antennas sticking up and a metal tray table.

The kitchen end was nothing more than a table for two, a small fridge, a stove with two burners and a sink. A washer and dryer crowded the only remaining space. The shack was messy and cluttered but clean, smelling of apple pie and wood smoke.

A fat red dog waddled from the single bedroom into the living space.

"She hasn't had those pups yet?" Bowie asked. He'd often wondered where and how she'd met the father of those pups.

"Sadie's like me. Takes her time. What's the hurry?"

Bowie bent to rub Sadie's floppy ears. An Irish setter, she was a beauty who followed her owner everywhere.

Jinx went into the kitchen section, motioning for Bowie

to follow. The plastic-covered pie and a pair of coffee cups were already set out on the tiny table.

Bowie chuckled. “You knew I’d come.”

“Eventually. Coffee’s always on.” Jinx poured them both a cup while Bowie scraped out a chair and sat. He’d had plenty of coffee already but figured another cup wouldn’t ruin him.

“What’s up?”

“Pie and coffee.” Jinx grinned through his beard, his teeth yellowed with time and too much coffee.

Bowie figured there was more to the cryptic summons than pie, but Jinx never rushed.

He forked a bite of the tender crust, the aroma of cinnamon and apples circling his nose and tickling his taste buds. The old man baked a fine pie, usually with whatever fruit he foraged in the woods. The apples came from the tree he’d planted when he’d first moved up here.

“How is it?”

Bowie chewed and swallowed, pretending to contemplate like a fine wine connoisseur. “Best I’ve had since the last one.”

“I figured all the girls in Sundown Valley kept you fed.”

“They do.”

Jinx’s thick brown eyebrows shot up. “Anyone in particular?”

Sage flashed in his head, but Bowie scoffed at the silly thought. She’d never fed him anything but her leftover French fries at Sonic. He didn’t even know if she could cook. Didn’t care either.

He had too much else on his mind.

“Ms. Bea, Cora Fletcher, Ellen Marsden to name a few.”

Jinx jabbed Bowie’s sleeve with his fork. “Every one of them is as old as me. I’m talking women your age, son.”

“I’m not. Great ladies. Want me to set you up with one of them?”

The old man laughed, long and loud, leaning back in his chair until Bowie thought he might tip over. When he’d finally settled back into place, he said, "Starting to worry about you, boy. Haven't you ever been in love?"

Bowie savored a sweet-tart bite of perfectly spiced apple before answering. "Thought I was once when I was a teenager."

"Ah. I remember now. The statuesque black-haired beauty who could run like the wind. What was her name?"

Run. That's what she'd done. Left him like too many others.

"Sage Walker."

"That's right. She moved away, didn't she? Is she the reason you're still single?"

Bowie took up his mug and used it to point at the other man. He was single by choice. Sage had nothing to do with his bachelor status.

"You didn't ask me up here to discuss my love life. Need me to pick up groceries? Haul off that old broken-down lawnmower. Or what?"

Jinx raised both hands in surrender. "All right. All right. I'll get to the point, though why a man wants to eat up all my pie and then run off, I'll never understand."

"Good pie."

Jinx laughed again and then sobered, leaning both elbows on the table. "Someone besides me is lurking around in these woods. I caught a glimpse of him a few times last week and again yesterday over near your place where you let me hunt. Closer to the lodge though. Skinny, hobo-looking fella."

"Probably a hunter staking out his tree stand or setting up his game cameras for the fall hunt." This time of year, hunters encroached on the Trudeau's wooded areas. He tried to keep them off, but the Sundown Ranch was big enough that the task was nearly impossible.

"My thought at first too, but my gut says different. I'll spot him out of the corner of my eye, but when I turn to get a better look, he disappears. Kind of like a wisp of smoke. He's there one minute and gone the next."

Bowie frowned, half worried, half amused. "You seeing things, Jinx?"

"Don't go thinking I've slipped a cog, will you? The visitor was real, but reclusive, careful-like as if scared of being discovered."

Another thought crossed Bowie's mind. The Keno family could be up to something, though why they'd come this deeply into the woods didn't make sense. Still, he wouldn't put anything past Bud and Bill Keno.

"Are you worried about being robbed?" Bowie would find a way to protect the old guy if necessary.

"You know better than that. I'm armed heavier than I was in the army." Jinx scratched at his beard. "But there's something familiar about the man that frets me. I just can't put my finger on it."

"We could set up some cameras of our own."

"Now that's a fine idea. You got any?"

None he could spare. With the Keno trouble ever brewing, he and Wade had security cameras in all the barns and outbuildings, as well as around the house. "I can get some."

With a nod, Jinx sat back and exhaled, long and deep. "That would relieve my mind."

Bowie's too. Jinx had never been one to exaggerate or to imagine things. If he thought someone was creeping around, he was probably right.

The worrisome question was who? And why?

A couple of hours later, with Jinx's grocery list in his pocket and his tools in the back of his truck, Bowie swung the big pickup truck into the only parking place available outside the Bea Sweet Bakery. The place was hopping this morning, the usual early morning rush. He tipped his hat to the banker, spoke to Rosalee Morales and her mother, and entered the cheerful conversational hum of Sundown

Valley's favorite morning ritual—sharing local news and hot doughnuts with good friends and neighbors.

Although he had no intention of looking for Sage, his eyes betrayed him. He spotted her in the kitchen, his eventual destination.

Right. She was still beautiful. So were lots of other women he knew.

To be certain he didn't let himself fall back into some youthful pattern of heading straight to Sage Walker, he lingered in the dining area to talk to Pastor Blake Cloud and the church deacons.

"Pull up a chair, Bowie, and give us your opinion on offering two services on Sunday, one contemporary and one traditional."

Bowie raised both hands. "Can't. I'm working on Ms. Bea's oven this morning."

"That old thing down again?" one of the deacons asked. "Why doesn't she get a new one?"

"Funds, I suppose." A small town bakery wasn't exactly a rich man's investment. "I can fix the old one." He took a step back. "Better get to it before she fires me."

The other three men laughed, as he'd intended. They all knew he didn't charge the widows a penny for his help. His aunt and uncle had cared for him when he was, for all intents and purposes, an orphan. The least he could do was pay it forward.

Wade claimed it was a compulsion, some inner need to make himself indispensable. He didn't like to ponder that too much. Lending a hand was the Christian thing to do. He wouldn't investigate the psychological implications.

With a nod to other friends and acquaintances, he started toward the counter. Ms. Bea was there moving as quickly as her arthritis would let her. Except for one or two, the customers didn't seem to mind the wait. Mornings were a time to linger with friends. Life moved slowly in Sundown Valley. People took time to know their neighbors and care about each other. It was one of the things he loved most about his little town.

"Morning, Bowie. How about a Bavarian cream?"

Although the smell of fresh, hot pastry set his taste buds aquiver, he patted his belly. "A friend filled me with pie."

"Someone trying to crowd me out?" Bea's eyes sparkled with humor.

"You're in no danger, Ms. Bea. But Jinx does make fine pie."

She laughed. "And I don't make any kind of pie these days. But if you get a hankering, give me a call." She winked. "I still know how."

"How's that oven this morning?"

"Old and cranky. Sometimes the rotator works, sometimes not. Sage has been watching it all morning, giving it a whack and a crank when it quits."

Sidling around her, he entered the kitchen. Next to the back door, Ryder and Paisley sat at the tiny table eating breakfast. Ryder glanced in his direction, suspicion clouding his eyes. Paisley gripped her lovey and stared at him. Both stopped eating, frozen like two scared rabbits.

Bowie couldn't take it. Caution was one thing. Fear was unacceptable. He went to them and crouched next to the table.

"Hey there," he said softly.

The children stared at him but didn't reply.

"Remember me?"

Ryder nodded. "You took us for ice cream."

"I sure did. You doing okay? That sausage and gravy smells good."

The little girl pushed her disposable plate toward him, eyes as round as the plate itself.

Heart pinched nearly in half, Bowie gently slid the food back to her. "Thank you, but I already had breakfast."

"Are you going to take us to the city?" Ryder asked,

his tone a tad belligerent. “My mama needs me. I have to go home.”

The child clearly didn’t understand the concept of two different cities. “No, buddy, I’m here to fix Ms. Bea’s oven if I can.”

The thin chest deflated. “Oh.”

Sage, who’d been frosting a pan of chocolate Long Johns when he’d entered the kitchen—not that he’d purposely noticed—came alongside him.

Hands to his knees, he pushed to a stand next to her. He’d always liked that she was nearly as tall as him, though she’d taken plenty of teasing in high school because of her height. Now, she wore heeled boots that brought her nearly eye level. Trendy boots, not Western wear, a reminder that her lifestyle was no longer small-town Oklahoma.

“Good morning.” A perfect smile lifted the corners of her full mouth. She looked tired, but as pretty as ever. If she wore makeup, he couldn’t tell. Hers was a natural beauty. Her hair pulled up in a messy bun, she wore a white baker’s apron over a pink T-shirt and skinny jeans that fit just right.

Weird that he should notice a woman’s clothes or hair. But no weirder than the surge of his pulse or the pure pleasure he took in looking at her. Like a work of art, her beauty was to be admired. Noticing didn’t mean he was falling under her spell again.

“Ms. Bea keeping you busy?” he asked, for lack of anything better to say.

“She worries me, Bowie. I wish I could do more.”

“She’s glad you’re here.” Which set up a swarm of other questions. Why *was* she here? How long would she stay?

Why couldn’t he stop thinking about her?

Irked at his wayward thoughts, he said, “I’ll look at that oven.”

“It should have cooled enough.”

He got busy troubleshooting the rotating device but

couldn't help listening in on the conversations between Sage and the kids and Ms. Bea, who occasionally wandered into the kitchen to see how things were going. Each time, Sage shooed her back to the chair someone had set up near the counter. Sage must have seen the need and insisted the baker sit down more often.

Frequently, his eyes strayed to the tall beauty as she bustled about the kitchen.

He guided them right back to the cranky oven rotator.

"Can we play out in the back, Aunt Sage?" Ryder slid off his chair and stood guard between his sister and the world.

Sage, about to carry a tray of fresh pastries to the display case, set it back down on the prep table.

Biting at her lower lip, she gazed from the kids to the back door. "I don't know, Ryder. Don't you want to color again today?"

"That's boring baby stuff."

Boys needed to move. Bowie knew that much. Being confined to a table in the back of the bakery would get old in a hurry. Was that all they'd done yesterday while Sage and Bea worked?

"I'm about finished here," he offered. "I could keep an eye on them for a little bit. Let them blow off some energy."

Sage got that look again, the one that both thrilled and embarrassed him for some troublesome reason. "No, no, Bowie. You have your own work to do."

She was right about that. He practically itched to get in his workshop and start playing around with ideas. But needy kids were his thing. According to his gut, Ryder and Paisley qualified.

"It'll wait." He gave the oven a metallic tap with his wrench. "Good as new." A grin overtook him. "Well, considering."

Sage tilted her head, green eyes sparkling. "Considering that it came over on the *Mayflower*?"

He pointed the wrench at her. "Don't tell Ms. Bea."

"Don't tell me what?" Bea shuffled into the kitchen. "That my equipment is older than Methuselah?"

Bowie exchanged an amused glance with Sage.

"Your oven is up and running smoothly, Ms. Bea," Bowie said. "I think I've fixed it, but if it quits again, call me."

"You're a blessing, a real godsend to this town, Bowie. Don't know what we would do without you."

Such compliments made him uncomfortable but pleased him too.

He didn't reply. Couldn't. He didn't know what to say.

He aimed his words at the two children watching the adults. "What do you think, kids? Ready for some outside time?"

Paisley was already out of her chair, dragging her lovey. Ryder watched Bowie for a long moment before sliding to an uncertain stand.

Bowie and Sage exchanged glances, this one filled with concern for the suspicious little boy.

Healing that kind of brokenness took time, commitment, and consistent effort by caring adults. Bowie knew that from personal experience.

And that worried him.

Was a restless heart like Sage able to give that to them? Would she even understand, as he did, how desperately they needed adults who cared enough to give them time and permanence?

An hour later, the morning rush subsided and Sage assisted in cleanup, wiping down tables, sweeping up and washing dishes while Ms. Bea served the slowed trickle of customers.

Frequently, Sage peeked out the back door to find the kids playing chase or building rock castles with the tall cowboy. Once, she'd heard Paisley laugh, a completely new and delightful event. Ryder, on the other hand, kept such a close watch on his sister that he was overly cautious even in play.

The anxious little boy opened a long jagged crack right down the middle of Sage's soul.

"He doesn't seem able to enjoy anything, does he?" Ms. Bea asked as she stepped up beside Sage to peer out at the children.

"I don't know how to help him, Ms. Bea. What can I do?"

Here was a woman who'd nurtured many broken children. If she didn't know, no one did.

"The social workers call his behavior hypervigilance. Whatever he's been through in the past has taught him that he can only depend on himself to keep him and Paisley safe. He feels he must always be on guard."

"That's a terrible thing for an eight-year-old."

"For anyone. But especially for a child." Ms. Bea placed a soft hand on Sage's arm. "He needs stability, Sage, and people in his life he can always trust."

"I know. I know." She gnawed her bottom lip, thinking, watching the handsome cowboy try his best to win the children's confidence.

Bowie glanced up, spotted her staring and lifted a hand. He spoke to the children and the three of them came toward the door.

"One thing for certain, you must get them into school," Ms. Bea said. "Ryder needs to focus on being a little boy with other kids his age. It will take his mind off guarding his sister every minute of the day. Paisley may blossom with other children too. Our school has some excellent counselors."

The idea of school set off an alarm in Sage's head. Schools needed records. They'd have questions. Someone might find a reason to contact authorities.

Heart jittery, she fell back on the only excuse she could think of. "Maybe it's best if I don't enroll them in school right now. I'm not sure how long we'll be here."

The older woman's kind face tightened. "You have to

do what's best for those children. Now, I'm not passing judgment. I don't know everything that's going on or that's gone on. If you choose not to tell me, that's fine and dandy. But you came to me and I've never been able to keep my opinion to myself when it comes to kids."

A slight smile edged up inside Sage's chest. "That's true."

For all her godly goodness, Ms. Bea was a tiger when it came to children.

"Whatever is going on, we can work it out. Right now, those kids need the consistency of school. They need to be learning."

Anxiety set up camp in Sage's belly and had a war dance. She couldn't risk telling anyone what she'd done. The kids were already wounded. They'd wither and die if they were separated from the only person left that they knew.

How could she let them begin school? She had no records, no guardianship papers, nothing to prove she had a right to have Ryder and Paisley in her possession. If the school got suspicious enough, they'd call social services. Or the police.

Then she'd have to take the kids and run. Again.

With her head and heart rattling, she ignored Ms. Bea's urgings by opening the back door for the trio. They came inside, disturbingly silent. The children returned to the little table like programmed robots. All three adults looked at them and then at each other with concern.

"Bowie," Bea said, "I was telling Sage that these kids need to be in school. You know the principal. Would you mind taking her down to the elementary to get them enrolled?"

Sage's pulse shot to Saturn level.

"No, Ms. Bea. No." Panic edged her words. "That's not necessary."

When the other two adults looked at her with puzzled expressions, she stammered out an excuse. "What I mean is, I can do it later myself. I don't want to trouble Bowie."

"What do you say, Bowie?" Ms. Bea pressed. "As a favor for an old friend?"

The cowboy rubbed a hand over the back of his neck. Reluctance hung on him like a cheap saddle. Couldn't Ms. Bea see that?

"I have a couple of things going right now…"

"Enrolling the kids won't take long. You know Mark. Sage doesn't."

"Right. Right." Bowie's soft eyes settled on Sage, calm and reassuring, as if he could read her inner panic.

He couldn't, of course. No way he could know the mess she was in. No way she could tell him, regardless of how trustworthy and solid her old friend was. Telling him one thing would lead to admitting everything else.

She already knew how he felt about druggies.

"It's no trouble, Sage," he offered quietly.

"There. The matter is settled." Bea rubbed her hands together. "Let's get these kids' hands and faces washed up and their hair combed and the four of you head on over to Sundown Elementary."

"But you need my help here," she argued.

Bea patted her shoulder again, this time in reassurance. "Honey, I appreciate all you do, but I've worked alone for years. I can handle another hour or two."

Without waiting for further argument, Bea gently guided the children to the little bathroom.

## *Chapter Six*

"They've built a new elementary school," Sage said as she and Bowie, the children between them, approached the long metal building with the giant eagle decal near the double front doors.

"About five years ago." Bowie stepped up to an intercom and pressed a button.

A disembodied female voice answered. "Hi Bowie. Come on in."

Sage shot him a look. He shrugged, a slight smile curving his mouth. "Small town."

Which could prove either good or bad. It was nice to be known, but it was also dangerous. She hoped no one remembered her that well, but she wasn't counting on it. Her height alone made her stand out.

A lock snicked and Bowie held the door while she and the kids entered. The distinctive smell of a school greeted her. Waxed floors, books, crayons, cleaning products. The tile floors gleamed beneath florescent lighting and shafts of sunshine. Brightly colored bulletin boards lined each side of the hallway.

Cheerful. Friendly. A safe place to learn.

She hoped.

Bowie pushed open a door on the right marked as the principal's office.

As if she wasn't nervous enough, two adults waiting in the reception area turned to stare. She saw curiosity from the woman and admiration from the man. Once, she'd enjoyed being stared at. Not anymore. Certainly not today.

Bowie nodded at the couple and, as if he felt her tension, squeezed her hand before stepping up to the counter. "Is Mark in?"

"He's with a parent, Bowie." The blond woman's name plate read Jocelyn Graves. Behind a pair of trendy red glasses, her eyes strayed from Bowie to the children, now jammed as close to each other as humanly possible. "Can I help you? Or would you rather wait for Mr. Feldman?"

"We need to enroll Ryder and Paisley—" He looked to Sage for their last name.

She swallowed, moving closer to give information. "Walker."

Amy had never married either of their fathers. Didn't even know where they were.

Jocelyn nodded. "I can help you with enrollment." She took two clipboards from a stack and handed them to Sage. "Fill out this information for each child, and we'll get you started."

"Thank you," she said, when what she really wanted to do was run out the door and escape before Jocelyn asked too many questions.

With courage she didn't know she had, she said, "I'm their aunt. I don't have all their information."

"Well, I'm not sure I can enroll them unless—"

The inner office opened and a woman exited. A man in a business suit, around Sage's age, followed. When his gaze fell on Bowie, a smile broke over his face. "Bowie. How's it going?"

The men exchanged handshakes.

"Come to talk school business or is this a social call?" the principal asked.

Jocelyn piped up. "His friend wants to enroll her niece and nephew, but she doesn't have all their paperwork."

The principal's gaze landed on the children. He smiled, an action that should have made her feel better but didn't. Beside her, Ryder stiffened.

With a motion toward the inner office, the principal said, "Come on in. We'll see what we can figure out."

The four of them followed the principal and settled in the armchairs across from a desk bearing a computer on one side and stacked everywhere else with folders and paperwork. Ryder and Paisley squeezed into the same chair, Paisley clinging to her lovey and her brother. Sage and Bowie bracketed them on each side.

The principal took his place in the leather executive chair, smoothed his blue and red Eagle's tie and perched his elbows on the desk, hands clasped.

He had a friendly expression below a shock of sandy hair and the kind of face that smiled a lot. Not that this relieved her mind one iota.

"Introduce me to your friend, Bowie."

"Sage Walker, meet Principal Mark Feldman. Mark, Sage."

The introduction was classic Bowie. Short, sweet, effective.

"Good to meet you, Sage. I take it you and these handsome children are new in Sundown Valley."

"I lived here years ago. I thought this would be a great place for the children. They've been through a lot." That much was true.

"What grades are they in?"

"I—" She didn't know. "I'm sorry. I just took custody of them." *Took* being the operative word. "Ryder is eight and Paisley is four, almost five."

"I see." The friendly face wrinkled into a contemplative frown. "So probably pre-K and second grade, if I'm guessing. We can call their former school and have their records faxed."

No. No, they couldn't. She couldn't take the chance that authorities could trace her here.

Sage cleared her throat. This was going just as badly as she feared.

"That won't be possible, sir," she managed. Her hands had begun to sweat and her belly quivered.

Bowie turned to look at her. The principal's frown deepened. Neither spoke, both awaiting her explanation.

"Home school," she blurted. "My sister moved a lot so she homeschooled the kids. They don't have any actual records."

"I see." Mr. Feldman rubbed a hand over his tie. The eagle claws rotated toward her as if eager to grab her by the throat and choke the whole story out of her.

Bowie spoke, quiet and easy. "Sage is trying to help these kids, Mark. I'll fill you in later, but can't we cut the red tape and do what's best for them right now?"

At that moment Sage wanted to hug the big cowboy. Fact was, she'd been tempted to hug him quite a few times over the past couple of days.

The principal nodded. "We run into this occasionally with homeschoolers. It's a bit of a problem, but not insurmountable." To Sage he said, "You fill out everything you can, and I'll take it from there."

Sage blinked three times before accepting that she was not about to be reported to child services or the police for kidnapping and impersonating a mother and whatever other crimes she may or may not have committed. The principal was serious. He was enrolling the kids in school, no further questions asked.

She must be dreaming.

Twenty minutes later the dream became a nightmare.

The four of them stood inside the pre-K class, a cheerful room where "London Bridge" played from a speaker and a dozen squirmy, giggling tots followed each other through the human tunnel.

When the sweet-faced teacher, Mrs. Prager, took Paisley's hand and encouraged her to join the fun, the child shrank back, shaking her head. Ryder, as always, moved in to block the adult from his sister. His small chest bowed out as if he was willing to take on all four adults if necessary.

It was heartrending. And Sage didn't know what to do. She placed a reassuring hand on Ryder's shoulder. On the other side, Bowie did the same.

She got that "want to hug him" feeling again.

"Give them a couple of minutes," Mr. Feldman said after he'd briefly explained the situation to Mrs. Prager. "We're in no rush. This is all new. Let them acclimate. If their aunt would like, she can take Paisley around the room and show her all the fun things she'll get to do in here."

Sage shot the man a grateful glance and reached for Paisley's hand. Without resistance the little girl followed her around the room. Ryder started to follow but Bowie said something to him and kept a light hand on his shoulder.

After a few minutes, Paisley began to touch objects in the various learning centers. Puzzles, art supplies, ABC blocks, all seemed foreign but fascinating to the child.

After a bit, a little girl in hot pink leggings and sparkle shoes came up to Paisley. "You can sit by me for the story."

Sure enough, Mrs. Prager was gathering the children into a circle on a brightly colored rug. Mother Goose characters marched around the perimeter and numbered squares made up the center. The teacher held a book in one hand and a puppet in the other.

"Ryder will be right down the hall, and I will be back after school to pick you up. You'll have fun. I promise."

Eyes wide, Paisley glanced toward her brother, but the

lure of the puppet was too much. She took the other child's hand and followed her to the rug.

Sage breathed a sigh of relief.

Everything seemed to be going well. Paisley sat down on the rug and only looked back one time.

When she was confident the child was settled, Sage returned to the doorway where Bowie and Ryder waited. Mr. Feldman motioned to them to follow.

"Second grade is across the hall and three doors down. Ready to meet your new teacher, Ryder?"

Ryder backed away, shaking his shaggy head. She *had* to get him a haircut. "I stay with Paisley. She gets scared."

"Paisley's fine. You can see her at lunch."

"Nuh-uh. I stay here."

"Ryder." Sage reached for his hand. "Come on now."

"No!" he yelled and yanked away. "No. I stay with my sister!" His voice rose on each syllable.

The principal quickly edged them into the hallway and closed the pre-K door.

Tears gathered in the little boy's eyes. He slashed at them. "She'll get hurt. I have to stay. Don't lock her in there. Don't lock her in there!"

He jerked away to pound on the door. With amazing reflexes Bowie caught him before the second strike.

Going to his haunches in front of Ryder, the tall cowboy held the boy by the shoulders. Ryder, stiff and shaking, looked as if he would either fight or crumple.

Tone as gentle and calm as a snowfall, Bowie said, "No one's locking anyone anywhere, buddy. Look." He reached and turned the doorknob. "Paisley wants to stay and play. She'll be safe. People here are nice." He winked. "And they have snacks."

"They'll let her eat?"

*Dear God, what had happened to these kids?*

"Yes. You too, although I don't think second grade has snacks," Bowie said.

"Hamburgers and fries for lunch today," Mr. Feldman put in. "And oatmeal cookies. How does that sound?"

Wild, uncertain eyes moved from adult to adult, seeking truth. It killed her, *killed her* to think of the weight this small boy carried on his shoulders.

"When can she come out?"

Ryder was back to worrying about his sister.

"Tell you what, buddy, maybe Mr. Feldman can ask your teacher to bring you down here a couple of extra times today to check on her for yourself."

Sage wanted to hug him again.

"We can do that," the principal said, his focus on the boy. "Will that make you feel better?"

Ryder nodded, though he didn't look too convinced. "Can I sit right here by the door until she comes out?"

"Why don't you try Mrs. Farmer's class first? She'll be your teacher and she's very nice." The principal patted Ryder's stiff shoulder. "I hear she hands out Scooby Snacks for good behavior."

"Okay." The frown on his face said he didn't believe a word of it, but with several backward glances, he followed them down the hall.

Bowie drove away from Sundown Elementary feeling as if a Clydesdale sat on his chest.

After getting the children settled in their classrooms, he and Sage had spoken privately with the principal about the situation, including Ryder's anxiety and Paisley's refusal to speak to anyone but her brother. Still, he didn't feel they'd done enough. They'd left a couple of frightened children with strangers and that bothered him.

Everything about those children bothered him.

As much as he wanted to keep an arm's length from Sage Walker, those kids ripped his heart right out of his chest.

Long ago, the Lord had placed it on his conscience and within his power to help needy kids. He'd done it for dozens of others in New Orleans and quite a few around Sundown Valley. If he had a life verse from the Bible, it would be James 1:7.

He let his own paraphrase of the verse roll through his head. True religion in God's view was taking care of widows and the fatherless. When those fatherless kids reminded him too much of himself, he had no choice but to commit.

He would do whatever it took to help Ryder and Paisley.

"Mr. Feldman seemed to care." Sage's voice broke through his thoughts. She was clearly fretting too.

Turned in the seat to face him, she leaned her back against the passenger door, dark hair shining in the autumn sunlight.

He heard the worry in her voice. She hadn't wanted to enroll the children. Maybe because of their apparent fears or because enrolling without records was complicated. More likely she wanted to remain footloose, free to leave if her restless soul took the notion.

Sage hated being tied down. How many times had she told him that in high school? She hated being in foster care. Hated being stuck in a place not of her choosing, which was the life of a foster kid, unfortunately, no matter how wonderful Bea and Ron had been.

He'd been far more fortunate.

He was glad he'd been able to run interference for the kids with the school. He suspected she hadn't told him everything about herself, about the kids and the life they'd been leading, and he wondered why. She'd once blurted out every secret, trusting he would never tell a soul.

Time, however, had a way of eroding friendships and

confidence. That's exactly what had happened to him. Older and wiser.

Yet, Sage needed a friend as much as those kids did. To help them, he'd have to guard his heart against her.

With all the work he had on his plate, he could do that.

"Mark's a great guy. That's why we hired him."

"We?"

He glanced her way and shrugged. "The school board."

"Of which you are a part?"

"Civic duty." He grinned. "No one else wanted to run."

"No wonder Mr. Feldman agreed to everything you said. You're his boss."

"I don't think of it like that. He's a friend first." He flipped on his blinker and made the turn toward the business section of town. "Mark will pull out all the stops to help Ryder and Paisley."

"I worry Ryder will try to run away again. He keeps talking about getting back to his mother."

"I noticed." He'd noticed too much. Ryder's obsession with his sister being locked in and his fears about having enough to eat. "And he's already tried to run once."

Sage must have been thinking the same thing because she said, "I don't know much about their lives, Bowie. I'd been in another state until Amy called me. Except for the occasional video chat, I hadn't seen them in a couple of years. Whatever went on could not have been good, but Ryder is not inclined to share information. When I ask, he clams up as if he'll get in trouble for talking."

"Maybe he would have." Harboring secrets, keeping his mouth shut, had been drilled into Bowie when he was small and on the streets with his mother. Ryder was likely the same.

"He thinks he's protecting Amy."

"Likely." Bowie pulled his truck to a stop at a red light. "You'd know about that, wouldn't you?"

He just looked at her, which was always pleasant, though the topic was not. Some things were still hard to discuss.

He'd guessed things about Ryder that Sage would never understand.

With that kind of terrible knowledge, he wasn't about to back away from the boy, no matter the personal cost.

At a corner table of the Bea Sweet Bakery, two older men each read a section of the *Sundown Valley Times*, their filled coffee cups in front of them. Sage didn't know the duo, but Bowie obviously did. As she and he entered the bakery, he stopped to say hello.

The man was nice to everyone. Just like before.

Though she remained concerned about her niece and nephew, her insides hummed from the morning's activities for reasons she couldn't quite nail down. Bowie's thoughtfulness, his caring manner with the kids, meant more to her than she could say. But more than gratitude heated a cold place in her chest.

Admiration.

Bowie Trudeau had grown into a man to admire.

Maybe he'd always been, and she'd been too self-focused to realize his value. He'd been her pal, the guy who was always there when she needed him. Though she was no longer a messed-up teenager, she'd fallen right back into depending on Bowie Trudeau. Easy. Comfortable. Bowie running interference on her ever-crooked life path.

Something else was going on too. Something she'd yet to put into its proper box.

A woman entered the bakery and Sage left thoughts of Bowie to turn her attention to work. Bea had gone to the back the minute Sage walked in, leaving her to run the counter. Bea treated her like a daughter, behaving as if she'd never left Sundown Valley.

Pleasure coursed through Sage. Unexpected. Fulfilling.

She waited on the customer, recognizing her as a former teacher, now retired. The two chatted, though Sage let Mrs. Marberry do most of the talking. It was better that way. Conversations could be tricky.

When the woman exited with a box of specially baked sugar-free cupcakes, Bowie came to the counter and said his goodbyes. Ms. Bea hollered from the kitchen. "Send that box in the warming case with Bowie."

Bowie chuckled, but, saying his usual nothing, accepted the white carton of goodies and left.

Sage watched his long muscled legs eat up the sidewalk between the bakery and his parking spot against the curb. Tossing his hat inside the truck cab, Bowie turned to look back, and when he saw her watching, lifted a hand.

Sage waved, feeling a little giddy to be caught watching him like some infatuated fifteen-year-old. She hoped he didn't think that.

Ms. Bea came up beside her. "That boy always cared for you."

"Bowie was once a good friend. I hope he will be again."

"That's not what I mean by caring, and you know it."

Sage laughed, though a little nervously. With her background and the uncertainty of what the future held, she couldn't let herself think of anything except friendship with the big cowboy.

Anyway, Ms. Bea was wrong. Bowie hadn't even wanted to go with her to the school. He'd only done it because he was a nice guy and Ms. Bea insisted.

Bowie had once been her best friend, but, then, he was everyone's best friend.

He drove all over town repairing ovens and water heaters and whatever any needy person required. He'd simply added her to his list of people to look after. She needed a friendly face. He'd provided one.

In fact, he'd probably be embarrassed to learn Bea thought he had romantic feelings toward her.

One of the men at the corner table lifted his cup toward the counter.

Bea motioned to her. "Refill Mr. James, would you, hon?"

Sage did as she was asked, returning with two empty sweet roll plates.

As she put the carafe back onto the heater, Ms. Bea asked, "You recall that horse Ron and I bought for you kids to ride?"

"Yes, I remember him. Chigger, wasn't it? He was such a sweet horse. Mr. Ron called him Chigger because he was small, only fourteen hands high."

Bea laughed. "Ron used to say your legs would drag the ground, but they didn't."

She'd learned to ride on that gentle little palomino. Many was the time Bowie had brought one of his horses into town and they'd ridden to the Sonic for a Coke or fries. Occasionally, he hauled Chigger and her to his ranch where they rode all afternoon.

They'd solved the problems of the world, hers anyway, on those idyllic days.

She wished life was that easy again.

As she carried the dirty dishes into the kitchen, she asked, "What ever happened to Chigger?"

He had to be really old. Was he even still alive?

"After Ron passed, I stopped fostering and had no use for a horse in my backyard. I put him up for sale." Bea took the plates from her hand and opened the dishwasher. "Guess who bought him?"

Sage reached for an empty display tray and plunked it into the suds-filled sink. "Who?"

"Bowie Trudeau." A plate rattled as she added it to the nearly filled dishwasher. "Now, ask yourself, why would a man with a ranch full of fine quarter horses and no kids pay too much money for a gentle little pony he didn't need and couldn't ride?"

"Bea, you're reading too much into it. Wade has kids now."

"He didn't when I sold the horse." She added another plate to the dishwasher, groaning a little as she bent. "If you ask me, Chigger reminded Bowie of the good times the two of you had together. He bought that horse to remember you."

Or maybe he'd bought the horse as a way to help Ms. Bea financially. Paying too much money for a kid's pony as a way to help a newly widowed woman was the kind of thing he'd do.

Ms. Bea was way off base on this one.

# *Chapter Seven*

By the time Sage picked up the children from school at three and returned to the bakery, the place was full of kids. Teenagers, preteens, elementary students who walked home from school. The building was a madhouse of jostling, laughing students there for an after-school snack and socializing.

No wonder Bea refused to close at noon every day. The school kids were a huge part of her income.

As Sage rushed around, waiting on the customers, Bea pointed out certain ones who required special foods because of health issues or allergies. A diabetic cupcake for the red-haired boy. Gluten free for two sisters. No peanuts or peanut butter for a cheerleader type with a toothpaste ad smile.

Bea knew every child and, as she'd done for Mrs. Marberry, created special treats for those who required them. Not one went away without a goodie in their hands. Even those short on funds.

Bea asked about their school day, their sick brother, the test they'd been worried about, all the while doling out treats and eats and making each child feel special. Feel *known*.

It occurred to Sage that the kids needed the bakery as much as the bakery needed their business.

After an hour of cheerful chaos, a daycare van pulled to the curb and half the kids rushed aboard, toting the remnants of their treats. Mothers and a few dads drifted in to talk amongst themselves and gather their offspring. Bea introduced Sage to all of them, many of whom she remembered. All of them were friendly, welcoming, expressing interest that she was back in Sundown Valley after such a long absence.

"Tomorrow you'll be the talk of the town." Bea hobbled past toting yet another white to-go box of pastries.

Tomorrow Sage and her niece and nephew would be food for the gossip mill. A curiosity. A reason for people to ask questions.

She tried not to let that bother her. Not today when she felt a part of something bigger than her problems. Not when she could forget her own worries and do something good for someone else. Wasn't that what being a Christian was all about? Doing good was certain to please the Lord.

Was that why Bowie played handyman for the townspeople? Was that why he was so kind to her?

The big, quiet cowboy had been a believer from the time she'd met him, solid in his faith, just as he was solid in everything.

He knew who he was and what he wanted in life.

She was still looking.

When the after-school crowd waned, she and Bea began cleanup. "I understand now why you don't want to leave the town without the bakery."

Bea wiped a sanitizing cloth over a table. "The business folks and senior citizens in the morning, the kids in the afternoon, and everyone else all day long, exchanging news and being good neighbors. It's what makes a community close. I thrive here."

"So does everyone else. This town needs the Bea Sweet."

"I can't argue that, but I need it too, honey. I'm not sure what I would do if I didn't have this bakery and my friends." She limped to the counter and headed into the kitchen. "Now, come on back here. We have time before the after-work crowd for me to show you how to test the dough and set up for tomorrow morning."

To humor her foster mom, Sage went along, though once she left Sundown Valley she'd have no reason to test dough or fill a hundred jelly doughnuts.

Inside his leather shop, Bowie sat at a makeshift desk sketching a flock of birds in flight above a mountain peak. In his mind's eye, he imagined the extra detail he'd add to create a beautiful, unique image on leather. Swirls and curlicues depicting wind and clouds, streaks to represent the sun's rays. Maybe some color here and there.

Was it unique enough for PJ Enterprises? Unique enough to grace the arm of a celebrity?

He pushed the paper aside, took out another, and began a butterfly design. So many ideas flooded his brain, everything from geometric and paisley to every animal known to man. Dragonflies, unicorns, even nautical and modern art.

He preferred crafting a scene rather than a single item, but considered his gift was in the detail, the coloring and shadows he added. He wanted his pieces to be distinctive enough that people recognized a piece as his.

His cell phone chimed. Deep in his art, he ignored it. A few minutes later, it chimed again.

With a sigh, he read the message. With another sigh, he left the leather and headed for his truck.

Though frustrated and more than a little concerned about making the December deadline, the ranch was his first responsibility. No one else even knew about his big dream. If he failed, the humiliation would be less painful.

The rest of the day he spent repairing a water gap in the north fence. It was an ongoing project, aggravated by the neighbors who weren't below sabotaging a good fence just for the fun of it.

The leather contract would have to wait. Though eager

to get on with the effort, he still had time as long as he stayed focused. Late nights were becoming the norm.

"I reckon we ought to scout out Keno's pasture to make sure we didn't lose a cow or two while this was down." Riley, their main ranch hand, motioned toward the land adjacent to the Sundown Ranch.

Keno land. Bad blood. If any of the four Keno males discovered a Trudeau brand on their property, they'd haul the animals to the sale faster than he could say goodbye.

"You brave enough to have a look?"

Riley laughed. "Does a frog bump his behind when he hops?"

In other words, yes. Cowboys didn't like their courage questioned.

"You finish up here. I'll have a look-see." Riley slithered his lean self between the barbed wires, through the low-water creek, and started across no-man's land. No-Trudeau land, anyway.

"Text or call if they start shooting."

Riley just laughed again. Bowie was serious.

By the time Riley returned, still alive to relate that he'd neither been shot at—a matter that seemed to disappoint him—nor had he seen a single animal bearing the Trudeau brand, Bowie had finished filling in the water gap and was ready to head to his workshop.

Finally.

As they mounted horses for the ride to the barns, Bowie said, "I visited Jinx again today."

"Yeah? He doing good?"

"As ever." Bowie shifted on the big, sturdy buckskin, Diesel, his favorite work mount. His boot slipped a little in the worn stirrup. The saddle needed TLC that would have to wait until he'd filled the contracted order. "A couple of times lately he's seen someone lurking around our property. Down near the canyon where we connect to the wilderness."

"Who was it?"

"He never gets a good look. Described him as tall and lean, dressed in camo but rough and ragged looking. Last time, he thought the man had a dog with him."

"Probably a hunter."

"That's what I thought, but Jinx seemed out of sorts about it. Uncomfortable. I told him I'd set up some cameras on his property when I get time."

Another thing on his agenda that he hadn't gotten around to.

"Couldn't be Kenos on that side of the ranch. Could it?"

Bowie arched his shoulders. "I don't put anything past that bunch."

"I could ride back in there when I get a minute, have a look if you like."

"Nah, just keep your eyes peeled."

By the time he reached the main house, Bowie put the stranger out of his thoughts. Sage and the kids, on the other hand, along with the art contract, had been in his head all day.

After a quick shower and hugs from the triplets, he glanced at the handyman list on his cell phone. He had only one stop tonight, mostly to make sure Fred Basil remembered to turn off his stove and feed his dogs. His daughter would be there during the day, but evenings were a challenge for the spry but forgetful octogenarian. One stop and then he could head back to the workshop and get in a few hours leatherwork.

Bowie answered a few texts, returned a couple of calls and then made one of his own.

He was about to hang up when Sage's husky voice said hello.

Bowie let the pleasure of her low voice sift through him like a warm drink on a chilly evening.

*Friends, Bowie. Friends.* Don't even let the other thoughts drift through your sappy head.

Getting left behind by people he loved hurt like a horse hoof to the midsection, no matter how much he enjoyed Sage's voice.

"Hey," he said. "How was today?"

"Good. Sorry I took so long to answer. Ms. Bea had my hands in dough, teaching me how to feel the proper elasticity."

He didn't know the first thing about dough. But a disturbing niggle of hope flared in a spot that refused to accept that Sage would never stick around.

"You learning to be a baker?"

She laughed. "No. I'm trying to be useful while I'm here."

While she was here. A few days in town and the restless heart was already planning her getaway.

Exactly the reason he would keep his heart out of this unexpected reunion.

Sage held the phone between her shoulder and her ear while she wiped bits of dough and flour from her hands with a white tea towel. The smell of yeasty dough circled her head, pleasant and homey. Heat rose from the oven where Ms. Bea's last batch of pastries for the day baked.

The rotator moved in a long, slow rhythm, working without a glitch.

"Bowie," she mouthed to Ms. Bea, indicating the caller.

Standing next to her at the prep table, Bea smiled her Cheshire cat grin and motioned for her to talk.

"This will wait," Bea whispered and pushed the dough away.

Sage fought not to roll her eyes. She wished her foster mom would stop. Bowie's purchase of a horse was a kindness to Bea and the animal, not a signal that he carried a torch for Sage. If he had, he'd have told her long ago. He'd have pursued her when she went to New York. He'd have kept in touch. That's what interested men did.

Bowie Trudeau was not interested, at least not in that way.

"How're the kids doing in school? Any issues?"

There. He'd called because of the kids, not her.

"Mr. Feldman came out to the Jeep today to speak with me. He said they do okay except that Ryder wants to run to the pre-K room every hour."

"Each day should get easier for them."

"I hope so. Paisley still doesn't talk to anyone, but when I asked if she likes her class, she nodded yes."

"Progress."

"Ryder isn't as excited."

"Give him time."

She prayed they *had* time.

Prayer. She wished she knew exactly how God worked. Sometimes her prayers seemed to float to the ceiling and linger there like so much hot air.

The line hummed between them, silent. Bowie talked more now than he did in high school but he still wasn't exactly a chatterbox.

"Well," he said, and she suspected he was about to hang up. She didn't want him to.

"Ms. Bea said you bought Chigger."

The line was quiet again.

Finally, he sighed, emitting a small chuckle. "Yeah. I guess I did."

"Why?"

"Seemed the right thing to do at the time."

He'd bought the horse to help Bea. He'd as much as admitted it.

Bea and her matchmaking skills were rusty. *Thank goodness.* Sage didn't need a boyfriend. She needed a friend. She needed Bowie. Like Bea, he was her connection to this town.

"How old is he now? Fifteen? Sixteen?"

"About that. He doesn't have papers but the vet puts him around that age."

"How's he doing?"

"Great. You'd never know his age by looking."

"Can I bring the kids to see him sometime? Maybe Saturday?"

The line buzzed quiet again.

Did he want to refuse?

"I think it would be good for the kids," she said, "but if you're busy—"

"Saturday's fine."

"In the afternoon, then? Ms. Bea needs me here in the morning."

Ms. Bea flapped both hands at her. "No, I don't. Go."

Sage turned her back to the woman. Bea had been good to her. She was going to do her part in this bakery.

"Are you sure you aren't too busy?" she asked once more to be sure she wasn't taking advantage of his kindness.

"No, no. Saturday afternoon works. See you then."

She heard a note of something in his tone that she didn't understand.

Or did Bea have her imagining things?

The rest of the week Bowie squeezed in only a few hours in the workshop. Between checking on the triplets, carrying both his load and Wade's on the ranch, and following up with every senior citizen on his to-do list, he was slammed. He'd even missed Bible study this week, something that rarely occurred.

He hoped things slowed down when Wade returned. They had to if he had any chance at all of making his deadline with PJ Enterprises.

Reining Diesel to a halt, he leaned on the saddle horn, rifle across the pommel, and surveyed a herd of young heifers.

Predators were ramping up for the winter. Young calves without a bull in the pasture were especially vulnerable. They'd lost one yesterday. He still hadn't found any sign of it.

This area of the ranch bordered the canyon, with forests on either end, and provided prime hiding spots for wildlife, both harmless and dangerous. Black bear, cougar, bobcat and coyote roamed these mountains and forests.

Using the exceptional field vision Uncle Brett had termed hunter's eyes, he scanned the landscape. Just inside the tree line, he spotted a doe and her twin fawns quietly grazing, a good indication that no predators lurked nearby.

Suddenly, the doe's nose jerked upward, winding the air. She and her offspring bolted. Diesel shifted beneath Bowie, ears pricked forward.

Except for a soft, calming murmur to the horse, Bowie remained perfectly still. Diesel settled.

Surrounded by the cattle, he and his mount blended in. Most likely, a predator wouldn't notice them at all.

Watchful, Bowie moved only his eyes, scanning, searching.

*There. Something.*

A movement. A flash like sun glinting off metal. A shadow.

Though far away, it looked more human than animal.

He reached for his binoculars. By the time he'd raised them to his face, the shadow was gone.

Was this Jinx's stranger? Or one of the Keno boys scouting for an opportunity to rustle a few head of Trudeau cattle?

Whoever and whatever lurked in these woods, the Trudeaus needed to be on high alert.

Yeah, like he had time to sit in the pasture and stare at the woods.

They'd have to move these calves closer to the house very soon. Another chore to add to his list.

After another ten watchful minutes, he looped the binoculars around his neck, and turned Diesel toward home.

With his mind never far from the contract he'd signed with PJ Enterprises, the doe had given him an idea for a sketch. Getting the time to execute that drawing was the hard part.

He'd planned to work all day Saturday in his shop. Now he was torn between fretting over artwork and Sage's planned visit. Saying no had been impossible. How could he refuse when he'd already promised himself and the Lord to do all in his power for Ryder and Paisley?

The bigger problem was, he looked forward to seeing Sage again way more than he wanted to allow.

Maybe he was more of a sucker than he thought.

The roads to the Sundown Ranch curved and switched back on themselves until Sage wasn't sure if she was coming or going. Literally.

Bowie had offered to drive into town and pick them up but she'd refused. Having her car gave her control. And after Bea's insinuations about her and Bowie, she definitely wanted to remain in control.

Bowie did not have a thing for her. He was just a do-gooder.

"Are we there yet?" Ryder asked, out of his seatbelt as usual.

"Soon." She gnawed her lip and glanced at the directions Bowie had given her. He'd laughed when she said GPS would guide her. Now, she understood. Cell phone service in these hills was not only spotty, it was nearly nonexistent.

"I'm pretty sure we take this road to the left." She signaled, though there wasn't another soul in sight. "Sit back and buckle up."

"We're lost, aren't we? We'll probably die. No one will ever find our bodies."

"We're not going to die, Ryder. We're going to ride horses. You'll love Chigger. He's the best horse. Your mom and I used to ride him when we were kids."

"I never rode a horse before."

"I know. Bowie will show you."

"Paisley's too little. She'll get hurt."

Sage flashed a look in the rearview mirror. She was pretty sure she heard Paisley whisper something to her brother.

"I won't let you," Ryder said to his sister. "Don't be scared."

Another whisper and Ryder said, "Yeah, I like him too. Kind of."

Who were they talking about? Bowie?

Just about the time Sage decided she was lost and would have to humiliate herself by somehow calling Bowie for rescue, she passed an orange gate with a no-trespassing sign.

She glanced at the written directions. Sure enough, he'd told her to drive past the orange gate another half mile.

Her text notification chimed.

At least *that* was working. For the moment.

Slowing the car, she broke another law and read the text.

Lost yet?

She laughed, shoulders relaxing. Leave it to Bowie to unknowingly make her feel better.

Her thumbs raced over the keyboard.

No!

You wouldn't admit it if you were.

Got that right, cowboy. I'm almost there.

Minutes later she pulled the Jeep down a long gravel drive beneath a Sundown Ranch cross timber. She remembered the place now, though it had been so long ago since her last visit, she'd forgotten the exact route. No one stumbled on the Sundown Ranch accidentally.

Bowie, in well-worn jeans and tan Roper boots, his solid red CINCH shirt open over a white tee, stood in the yard waiting for them.

Had she ever before noticed how good his dark skin looked in red?

*Ms. Bea, what have you done to my head?*

When he lifted a hand in greeting, his watch caught the sunlight, drawing her eye to the intricate leather watchband. She'd noticed the beautifully tooled bracelet before, but now she wondered if he'd made it, if he still played around with leather crafting.

She parked and the three of them tumbled out.

Ryder, the smarty, marched right up to Bowie and said, "She got lost."

Bowie's gaze met hers, coffee-brown eyes dancing.

"We weren't lost. We were...exploring."

He grinned and, with a wink, whispered to Ryder. "She was lost."

Shockingly, Ryder returned the grin. It was the first smile she'd seen out of the solemn child.

Sage perched a hand on one hip, pretending insult. "Are you guys ganging up on me?"

Bowie, who'd apparently noticed the improvement in Ryder's attitude, kept up the banter. "Us men stick together. Right, Ryder?"

Paisley edged up close to her brother, lovey at her cheek.

Ryder's expression darkened. He took her hand. "Paisley too."

The adults exchanged looks, this one of concern. The boy worried even when joking.

"How about this?" Sage said. "We'll all stick together today. All for one and one for all."

This seemed to appease the child and, holding to Paisley as if he feared she'd be kidnapped, he fell into step next to Bowie as they headed toward a barn.

*Please Lord, show me how to help Ryder. Teach him how to relax and be a little boy.*

She'd do anything to make things better.

Bowie pondered his visitors as they walked the distance from the house to barn 1. These past three days Sage had been on his mind too much. He kept thinking about today's visit, about spending time with her again. He hadn't intended to, but at every turn, she jumped into his head.

He'd phoned her a couple of times to see if she needed anything but hadn't stopped at the bakery. Temptation tried to pull him in, but fortunately, he'd been too busy to drive into town.

Wade had made his usual video call to the triplets last night while Bowie was at the main house. They'd talked business for a bit, but the man was on his honeymoon. Bowie wasn't about to share any problems, including the concern that the Kenos were up to no good again.

Instead, he'd mentioned Sage's return to Sundown Valley along with other cheerful news of the town and church.

If Wade remembered the mad crush he'd once had on Sage, he didn't mention it. He was, however, happy to learn Ms. Bea now had a full-time assistant at the bakery. A temporary worker, he said, was better than nothing.

Bowie slid a glance at his guest, in total agreement with his cousin. Ms. Bea needed her. The kids needed Ms.

Bea and Sundown Valley. Sage probably did, too, though Bowie was too cautious to pry into the last thirteen years of her life.

"The ranch looks different." Sage stopped on the gravel path and turned in a circle.

"Really?" Bowie glanced around, trying to see the place through her eyes. "How?"

"You've built more barns, cleared a line of woods that was there." She pointed toward the west. "Planted fruit trees."

"We did that a long time ago. Trent loved peaches and every year during fruit season, he wished for a peach tree. After he died…"

Touched, she reached for his hand and squeezed the way he'd done for her on the first day of school. "I understand."

For a nanosecond, he enjoyed the feel of her cool, smooth skin against his. Then, with an inner growl of chastisement, he let go.

"Trent's Orchard, we call it."

"A living memorial."

He'd known Sage would get it. She was intuitive that way or had been in high school. Except when it had come to his feelings for her. Then she'd been dense as a railroad tie. In retrospect, maybe that had been a good thing.

He'd be a friend, but he refused to let his heart get tangled up with someone with leaving on her mind.

Besides, he was an adult now, not an awkward boy with a crush. He dated. Had lots of friends, girls and guys. Nothing serious, but he wasn't a hermit like Jinx who'd given up on life.

Someday he'd find the right woman. A godly, steadfast woman like Kyra who had permanence tattooed on her heart; not a roamer.

Just because he liked Sage and wanted to spend time with her didn't mean he was foolish enough to fall for her again.

The barn door squeaked, metal on metal, as he rolled it open. Blinking against the dimness, they stepped inside. Bowie breathed in the smells of hay and sweet feed and the gathered equines. He was born for this kind of life. Even horse manure smelled friendly to him.

Another reminder of the kind of woman he wanted. Someday.

"I brought the horses in from the pasture this morning and worked them out. They should be ready for visitors."

He'd risen early, way before dawn to squeeze in two hours in the workshop. At daylight, he'd saddled Diesel, checked the nearby herds and gathered the horses.

The children stood wide-eyed, staring at the big equine heads hanging over stall doors. Sage spotted Chigger right away and hurried to him.

"Bowie. It's Chigger! He looks wonderful." She reached for the palomino's halter with one hand and stroked the golden muzzle with the other. "Hi, friend. Remember me?"

Chigger, more dog than horse, loved to be petted. He turned soft, adoring eyes on the woman.

"Look, Bowie, he knows me."

Bowie just smiled. Maybe he did. Bowie wouldn't argue. Horses were smart.

"You kids want to pet the horse?" Bowie asked.

Ryder's worried gaze was locked on Sage and Chigger. "Will he bite me?"

"Is he biting Sage?"

Ryder gave that some thought. Then, with Paisley clinging like a sticker burr, he edged up to the stall and extended a hand.

Sage wisely guided the little fingers to the horse's neck.

Wonder replaced Ryder's worry. "He's soft. Feel him, sissy."

With confidence, thanks to her brother, Paisley rubbed Chigger's neck. Sage held the halter, keeping the animal still.

Bowie moved down the line of horses, stroking, talking softly. He was aware of every move the children and the woman made. Especially the woman.

Having Sage here on the Sundown felt right. Naturally, when he looked at her, he saw her exceptional beauty. A man would be blind not to notice. But more than her beauty, he saw the girl who'd once considered him her best friend. The girl who'd called him when she was happy, when she was sad, when the restlessness compelled her to do something crazy.

Long ago, this ranch and their friendship had been enough to settle her restless soul. Until it wasn't.

"Can we ride him?" Ryder asked with sudden bravado.

Bowie left his horse and his musings to join the trio at Chigger's stall.

Sage turned her face up to him. It didn't take much. She wore the same fashionable heeled boots again, bringing them nearly eye to eye.

"How about letting them sit on Chigger," she said, "while you lead him in the round pen. I'll walk next to them."

"You don't want to ride?"

"Maybe later if they want to. We'll double up. You with one of the kids. Me with the other."

Casting a long gaze down the road toward the workshop he couldn't see from here, Bowie nodded.

The kids needed this. Work would wait.

# *Chapter Eight*

Two hours later, with the warm autumn sun on their backs and a soft southern wind in their faces, they ambled two horses through the still-green pastures.

Through gates that Bowie opened from atop his horse, over hills, across small trickling creeks where fat, shiny black cattle dotted the countryside, they rode, sometimes talking, sometimes silent.

Sage was glad Bowie had invited her. Except he hadn't exactly. She'd invited herself. She recalled his brief hesitation on the other end of the phone. Had he minded? Did he have other plans? Were they imposing?

She slid a glance toward her companion. He rode the buckskin horse as he did everything, relaxed, in control, quietly accepting whatever came his way. If he objected to her visit, he'd never tell her.

Ryder sat in front of the rancher, eyes wide, taking in every cow and horse, pointing out the baby calves, in awe of being in the country.

She and Paisley rode Chigger. Half asleep from the gentle rocking motion of the horse's smooth gait, Paisley snuggled against Sage's torso, clutching the ever-present lovey.

"Have you ever been on a ranch before, Ryder?" Sage asked.

"No. Paisley neither."

That explained their interest as well as their hesitancy.

"What do you think? Do you like it?" Bowie shifted slightly, one arm around the boy, letting the reins rest in the opposite hand. His horse seemed to respond to the slightest twitch of the reins or movement of his strong legs.

Chigger readily followed Bowie's horse, a buckskin he called Diesel.

"I like it. Maybe I'll be a cowboy when I grow up."

Bowie said nothing, but his smile set his chin dimple into action. She found herself drawn to that smile, to his handsome face, to those kind, kind eyes.

Truth was, she found herself drawn to the man himself.

But hadn't she always been? Except this time felt different. This time they were adults.

She shook her head and looked away from the man, more than a little disturbed at her wayward thoughts.

Ms. Bea had put ideas into her head. Bowie didn't care for her that way. Even if she wanted him to, Bowie was a straight shooter, the boy who never got into trouble, the man who did only good.

Though she was a Christian now, trying to do the right things and often failing, she'd never been called good. Bowie would spur his buckskin horse and ride like the wind if he knew the trail of mistakes she'd left behind.

"I want to show you something," he said. "Remember the canyon?"

Bowie's voice brought her right back to looking at him. "Vaguely."

With a gentle twitch of the reins, Diesel veered to the right, turning them westward. Chigger followed. The steady old horse didn't need direction from her. He knew what to do.

Bowie led them along a creek and through a dappled stand of brush and trees. As they came out on the other side, a long, narrow canyon stretched below them. At its bottom, the twisting creek they'd crossed earlier widened, flowing over rocks and fallen timber.

Bowie rode Diesel up to the five-strand fence erected, no doubt, to keep cattle from tumbling off the edge.

He dismounted, lifted Ryder down and then came for Paisley. When he reached back for her, Sage thought nothing of sliding into his arms. Nothing until they were chest to chest, faces so near she noticed a tiny scar below Bowie's left eye. Tempted to touch it, to touch him, she gave an awkward chuckle and took one step back.

Bowie dropped his hold on her waist, a soft smile on his lips.

Ms. Bea and her innuendoes. *Really.*

"Legs tired?"

*Of course.* The ride was why her knees trembled. "I haven't been on a horse since I was here last."

"You still run?"

"Every day." Which meant her legs should be strong. She gave another laugh, this one self-deprecating. "I should be in better shape."

"Riding's a different set of muscles."

Another man would have mentioned her shape, probably complimented or said something suggestive. Not Bowie.

Which proved how wrong Ms. Bea was.

"Are you saying I'll be sore tomorrow?"

A sparkle lit his dark eyes. "In places you forgot you had."

He took Chigger's reins from her and tethered both animals to a sapling. The horses dropped their heads to graze on the ankle-high grass.

Hands in her back jeans pockets, Sage joined the kids near the fence. Both had scampered up to the canyon's edge the minute Bowie stood them on the grass.

Bowie's canyon wasn't particularly wide nor grand, nor was it layer upon layer of colorful rocks as in the Palo Duro. Plants grew here. Vegetation in a shout of fall colors spread down the sloping land toward the dancing creek, a carpet of green, red, orange, yellow and gold.

"So pretty," she said.

"Just wait ten minutes. It gets better." She heard the smile in his voice.

The kids soon grew antsy and wandered away from the canyon's edge to race through the grass and around trees.

She turned to the side to watch them. Ryder seemed like an ordinary eight-year-old out here in the country, running free.

"They're okay," Bowie reassured her.

"Yes. I think they are."

The two of them began to talk then. Her mostly. About old times, funny remembrances and the changes in the world since they'd last ridden together. She told him about the townspeople she'd become reacquainted with, and they rehashed their concerns about Ms. Bea's health and the bakery. He told her about his group of friends and invited her to church and the dinner planned for afterward.

Pointing to his watch, she asked about his leatherwork and was not surprised to learn he'd built a workshop dedicated to his art.

She told him about the one guy she'd dated seriously for about a year, leaving out all the losers and users. When he didn't reciprocate, she wondered if someone had broken his heart. She didn't ask though. Bowie would tell her if he wanted her to know. Wouldn't he?

Or was she leaning too heavily on their long-ago relationship?

The conversation lulled occasionally but the quiet was comfortable, like Bowie. Quiet was his nature.

"You blend with the outdoors," she told him. "Like you're part of it."

That soft smile again as he turned his head toward her.

"Maybe I am. What about you, Sage? What are you a part of?"

The innocent question reopened the uncertainty, the longing that had plagued her forever. She raised a shoulder. "I don't know. Still looking, I guess."

"For the end of the rainbow?" His tone was half amused and half serious.

The tumultuous need to find something that she could not describe followed her wherever she landed. She knew she was restless, unsatisfied, always searching. She didn't want to be. She just was.

"It's got to be out there somewhere. The place I'm supposed to be. The thing I'm supposed to do with my life."

"Have you asked God?"

That he discussed his faith so easily didn't surprise or offend her. Easy was his way.

"Not really."

He didn't push or tell her that she should. She was grateful for that. She was still learning how to navigate the lifestyle she read about in her Bible.

When she'd been a teen, living with the Cunninghams, they'd taken her to church and had lived their faith in front of her. Uninterested then, she'd mostly ignored the lessons.

Only in her darkest hour had she remembered there was a God. Only when she had nothing and no one left to call upon had she reached out to the One who Bea had promised would stick closer than a brother.

She felt guilty about that. Would God hold it against her that she'd only come to Him in desperation?

She didn't know. Didn't want to ask in case the answer was yes.

As they walked along the canyon edge, the children darted around them, playing, gathering rocks and rushing to her with the occasional acorn or bird feather.

"The wonders of the country." Sage smiled when Bowie stuck a blue feather in her hair.

"If you keep looking," Bowie said to the children, "you might even find an arrowhead."

Ryder frowned. Though she'd trimmed his bangs his sandy hair stuck up in a dozen directions, endearingly ruffled by rambunctious play and a south wind. "What's an arrowhead?"

"The end point of an arrow. You've seen a bow and arrow before, haven't you?"

"Yeah. On TV. Are they real?"

"They are. People still hunt with them. But the arrowheads you'll find out here are very old and made by hand."

"How?"

"A long time ago, native tribes like the Caddo and Choctaw used to hunt this area. They didn't have stores, so they made their own arrowheads from stones or animal bones."

"That's pretty cool."

"Very. Finding one is a rare and special gift."

"Come on, Paisley. Let's find an arrowhead." Ryder started to rush away and then turned back. "What do they look like?"

Bowie didn't laugh or tease, as some would have. Serious and patient, he took a stick and traced a shape on the ground.

Ryder rushed away, Paisley trotted behind, searching the grass for more treasures.

"You've captured his interest. Thank you."

"I hope he finds one," he said, watching the now-animated child.

"Me too."

Suddenly, she stopped and grabbed Bowie's forearm.

His head jerked toward her. "What is it?"

"I thought I saw someone." She pointed. "There. In those trees."

A scowl plowed furrows in his forehead. He stared in the direction she pointed. "Where exactly?"

"I don't see anything now. Maybe it was a shadow. Or an animal."

"Possibly." But he continued to stare at the line of woods across the canyon, his eyebrows plunged close together.

"It's getting late," she said when nothing else moved and she felt a little silly for saying anything. "The sun is about to set."

"Uh-huh." Bowie didn't seem in the least hurry. He turned his attention away from the woods and the person who probably hadn't even been there. "A couple more minutes."

"You can find your way home in the dark?"

The spokes around his eyes deepened. "If I can't, Diesel and Chigger can."

"I didn't know horses could see at night."

"Now you know." His low chuckle sent a pleasant tingle up her arms. She rubbed at them, content in a way she hadn't been in a long time.

She credited the beauty of outdoors in the autumn. Nature was incredibly healing for the mind and spirit. She needed to get out into the country more.

Her gaze found the kids, frolicking and laughing and tossing handfuls of grass into the air. They needed the same.

She had Bowie to thank for this. Being with him, here on his huge ranch, eased the tightrope that seemed to be wrapped around her chest.

For the sake of the children, she'd ask if they could come again.

The air began to cool and the wind died to nothing as the sun slowly slipped toward the horizon.

Bowie pointed upward. Silhouetted against the faded

denim sky, a red-tailed hawk circled in a last ditch attempt at finding tonight's dinner.

As she watched the bird, his wings spread in an easy soar, the landscape took on a golden glow.

Grasping Bowie's wrist, she gasped and pointed toward the west. "Bowie. Oh, my."

"I thought you'd like it. The golden hour, photographers call it."

So this was why he wanted to wait.

Along the canyon walls, the colors deepened as the sun made its descent, casting a golden hue over everything. On the horizon's edge, the stunningly red-orange sun shot beams across the mountains, setting them in purple and blue shadow. Before her eyes, color spread in all directions, turning the sky unnamable shades of coral, yellow, red and gold, blues and purple.

"It's glorious." She spoke in hushed tones, awed. "The prettiest I've ever seen."

"This place," he said, his voice matching hers, "reminds me of how ancient our land is, of how God created all of this out of nothing, and that it only belongs to us for a little while. Like the natives before us who stood on this very cliff and watched the sunset—we're stewards, not owners. God owns this. Yet, He lets us enjoy it."

Sage moved closer to him, impressed by the number of words he'd strung together and aware that she'd once again twined her fingers with his. The way they used to do. When they'd been teenagers.

"You can almost hear the echo of long-ago natives singing around their campfires."

He glanced at her in quiet approval. "And smell their wood smoke."

Slowly, majestically, the sun melted behind the mountains, multicolored crayons fusing together. The glow covered the land, gilded their faces, bringing a tranquility she was hard-pressed to explain.

For this brief interlude when the world seemed beautiful, and Bowie stood at her side holding her to this place, peace settled over Sage as surely as purple dusk settled over the mountains.

She'd done the right thing by returning to Sundown Valley.

Bowie glanced down as if only just noticing their clasped hands. He moved as if to release his grip, but Sage held on.

She wasn't ready yet to end this near-spiritual moment.

Their eyes met. Something sparked inside her.

They were standing close but she shifted closer so that their sides touched. Bowie was warm, steady, strong. As they watched the sun disappear behind the mountains, she leaned her head on his shoulder and sighed.

"I'm glad you're my friend. You're a good person, Bowie Trudeau."

"So are you, Sage Walker."

She wanted that to be true. But she was very afraid it wasn't.

Back at the main house a short time later, Mrs. Roberta fed them tacos before they adjourned to the living room where the triplets entertained Ryder and Paisley and had them laughing.

Bowie had to admit, the afternoon had been nearly perfect.

Regardless of the contract pecking at the back of his brain, regardless of his vow to maintain a distance from Sage, he'd enjoyed today.

He feared he might be losing ground in his battle to hold her at arm's length.

"You still want to see my workshop?" He shouldn't have

said that, shouldn't have urged her to stay any longer, but he wanted her to.

*Foolish heart, don't do this to me.*

"Absolutely. A peek anyway. We have to get home soon." She glanced at Paisley. The little girl sat on a rug, staring at her brother and the triplets, unmoving, too tired to play anymore.

"His shop's cool, Aunt Sage." Ryder hopped up from playing cars with Ben and Caden. "Bowie makes wallets!"

"Super cool. Let's go have a look."

A few minutes later, they were in the shop. Ryder, behaving as if he'd been there a dozen times instead of as a stowaway only once, marched up to a worktable.

He turned to Bowie. "Where's the wallet?"

"Finished." Bowie reached up to a shelf above the worktable and took down a shoebox. "Here it is. What do you think?"

"Wow." Ryder traced a finger over an intricate horse head design. "He looks real."

Inside the shoebox were a few more completed pieces he'd promised to friends.

Now that these items were finished, he could fully concentrate on the designs for PJ Enterprises.

Though he'd drawn and cut out two projects for the contract, he kept those out of sight in a special container, waiting to find the time to tool the designs.

Those had been on his original agenda for today.

"He's supposed to look real." Bowie set the box on a low table so Sage and the children could look. He rarely let anyone see his work until it was finished. It was just a quirk he had, especially now that he'd committed to creating something special and new.

The horse head wallet, modeled after the photo of the purchaser's own horse, was joined by a belt braided along the edges and inset with turquoise and silver, three bracelet sets, a watchband similar to his, and an engraved dog collar.

"They're beautiful, Bowie. What will you do with them?"

"I made these for a friend in Colorado. Christmas gifts for his family." He could have reneged on the promised gifts. Jim would have understood considering he was the one who'd recommended Bowie to Katherine Pembroke, but reneging wasn't his way. A man, as he'd told Ryder, was only as good as his word.

"Including the dog?"

He grinned. "Even Butch, the boxer."

"I had no idea you were this good. These are exquisite. The detail..." She practically breathed the final words.

Her comment gratified him every bit as much as Katherine Pembroke's praise and the amount of money he was hoping to earn. He smiled, but said nothing.

A man shouldn't boast. Let the work speak for itself. That's what his uncle had taught him and the advice had stood him in good stead.

Ryder slid a fingertip over the name he'd tooled into the belt. "Can you make me something?"

"Ryder," Sage admonished. "It's not polite to ask for things."

"Oh." Ryder clammed up, his face closed and uncertain again. The little guy seemed to shrink into himself.

That wouldn't do. Bowie didn't want to stand in the way of Sage's authority but anytime the boy showed interest, it was important to encourage him. Uncle Brett had done that for Bowie when he'd shown an interest in training horses. The resulting affinity with the animals had healed huge chunks of his soul.

"I have something to show you, Ryder."

The little guy looked at him with suspicious eyes. Paisley moved closer, as if aware of her brother's sudden negative mood. She pushed her lovey against his cheek.

The action chipped a piece of Bowie's heart.

Taking down another, much smaller box, he removed an item. "You want to see an arrowhead?"

Both Ryder and Paisley had been disappointed not to find one. He was disappointed for them.

"A real one?"

"I found it myself down in the canyon by the creek."

Ryder opened his hand to receive the small treasure.

"Just think, buddy. Long ago, a man or maybe a boy like you, found this bit of flint rock and chipped away at it with another stone until he'd carved it into this shape."

"Do you think he shot a bear with it?"

"Maybe. For sure, he shot at something or he wouldn't have lost his arrowhead for me to find all these many years later."

Ryder traced the shape, flipped the piece over and examined every groove and curve. "Maybe someday I'll find one."

When he started to hand the arrowhead back, Bowie closed the little fingers around it. "Keep it. But take care of it. Never lose it. A real arrowhead is irreplaceable."

He didn't know if the boy knew the meaning of the word, but his solemn nod said he got the message.

"Thanks, Bowie."

Though he wanted to linger and show them everything, the day was gone. The kids were tired. The fun was over. Paisley had begun to sag against her brother, eyes drooping.

And he planned a few hours of leather crafting tonight.

He took them back to the house and walked them to Sage's Jeep, helped buckle the kids inside and then stood in the opening of the driver's door for a final goodbye.

"Church tomorrow? You can ride with me if that makes going easier."

"What time?"

"Sunday School at 9:30. Church at 11:00. Both or either. Your choice."

"Both."

The answer thrilled him to his boot toes.

Before he could march out all the reminders of why he shouldn't touch her, he cupped Sage's cheek. Her hand went to his waist.

Suddenly, surprisingly, the air hummed.

In the light of a white moon bolstered by the ranch's security lights and the Jeep's cargo light, they were half in shadow.

His pulse quickened. *Sage,* he thought. *Sage.*

*Oh, man. He was in trouble.*

While he fought not to do anything ridiculous, like kiss her, Sage took hold of his wrist and turned her face into his hand, pressing her lips against his palm.

"Good night, Bowie. Thank you for today."

Unable to speak, he nodded and stepped back, closing her car door with a firm snick.

Then he stood in the darkness and watched her drive away, fingers curled over the place where her soft, warm lips had touched his skin.

Maybe he wasn't over Sage Walker, after all.

# *Chapter Nine*

She'd wanted Bowie to kiss her. Had she lost her mind?

Sage banged a cleaned and sanitized pastry tray onto the rack and slammed another on top of it.

She couldn't believe she'd done something as dumb as kissing his hand.

She rolled her eyes. For crying out loud. Who kissed a man's hand?

Not just any man's hand. Bowie's. Her buddy. Her pal.

And now, tomorrow, she'd attend church with him.

Maybe she was just tired. That was the only excuse she had for doing such a ridiculous thing.

After tucking Ryder and Paisley into bed and leaving Ms. Bea to watch over them, she'd come to the bakery to finish the cleanup from this morning. Saturdays were hectic, she'd learned very quickly. And she'd made Ms. Bea promise to go home, put her feet up and take a nap at closing time, leaving the cleanup for Sage.

That Bea had agreed so easily fretted Sage no little amount. It was out of character. Bea must be in more pain than she let on.

After sanitizing all the trays, she started cleaning the rest of the shop. All the while, her mind whirled. She jumped from the hand kiss to the wonderful afternoon. The kids had loved it. She had loved it. They'd all needed it. And if she wasn't mistaken, Bowie had a good time too.

So, why was she twisted up like a cinnamon stick over an innocent show of affection to an old friend who'd gone out of his way to help her and the children and to make her feel welcome?

Because today had felt like more than friendship.

Monday morning the business crowd was back in the bakery, ordering up light breakfast fare, fresh, hot coffee and juice. Dozens of warm doughnuts, muffins, cinnamon rolls went out the door in white boxes. The smell of baked goods rolled out the front doors, enticing townsfolk to begin their workweek with coffee and community.

Busy trying to take the load off Ms. Bea who'd been up since four o'clock, Sage found herself swept up in the town chatter and the local news circling through the bakery like the scent of cinnamon. Jessica Swanson had twin girls over the weekend. Ms. Bea was packing her a box of pink iced cookies. Bert Thomson was home from the hospital again. Diabetic banana muffins for him. Shane and Alice Walkingstick had moved into their new home on his Choctaw land. For their housewarming, a baker's dozen lettered cupcakes that spelled out Home Sweet Home.

As Sage dashed into the kitchen for another tray of sprinkled doughnuts, she slowed to watch Bea add the final touches on the housewarming cupcakes. "Do you do this every Monday?"

Bea gave her a tired smile. "These are all friends and good customers. Don't scold, Sage. I love doing it."

Ms. Bea was a giver. It was one of the things Sage loved about her. It was the very reason Bea had taken Sage into her home years ago and again this month.

Sage wiggled a finger toward the pretty pastel lettering atop a cupcake. "Teach me how to do this so I can help you."

The tired face lit up, accenting age lines. "Oh, hon, that would be wonderful."

In between customers and refills, Bea taught her the

finer points of fancy frosting. The process was, Sage discovered, not as easy as it looked.

Motioning to her kindergarten scrawl of crooked letters, she laughed. "Mine will never be presentable."

"Sure they will. Persistence, honey. Keep practicing on the clean cookie sheets, scoop up the mistakes and use them to practice again. You'll get it."

Persistence. Something that had been sorely lacking in her life. If the going got tough, this tough girl got going… somewhere else.

By the time the afternoon crowd hit, Sage was surprised to have mastered the rudiments of fancy icing, stars, letters and rosebuds. She already knew how to add the regular glazes to the various pastries and was getting better at knowing when a bowl or tray was properly proofed and ready to transform into delicious sweets. She'd fried doughnuts when she was in high school and knew how to keep the display cases clean and filled.

Knowing she could do these things for Ms. Bea gave her a sense of satisfaction. She was earning her keep. The more her healthy, fit body could do, the more Ms. Bea could rest and let her swollen knees and feet recover.

Late that afternoon, when the first trickle of elementary students began arriving with their mothers, a short redhead entered. The familiar-looking woman held the hand of a boy around Ryder's age.

Sage stepped to the counter and smiled. "How may I help you?"

The redhead stared at her for a few blinks. "Sage? Sage Walker? Do you remember me? Hannah used-to-be Mayfield. I'm Hannah Redding now. This is my son, Patrick."

She did remember. Hannah had sat next to her in history. They'd done an American Revolution project together. Hannah had been one of the nice girls.

"Hannah. Hi. You married Joel Redding, the class president. Right?"

Hannah hooked a lock of straight hair behind one ear. "I did. And he's as smart as ever. A lawyer and, get this, the mayor now, if you can imagine."

"We all knew he'd be a success."

"What about you, Sage? We expected to see your face splashed in every magazine and TV ad."

Keeping her expression smooth, she answered with her usual line. "I wasn't cut out for that life, I guess." She forced a chuckle. "Too much dieting!"

Truth. Just not the whole truth. Her past was her business.

She wished social services agreed.

"After having Ms. Bea's cinnamon rolls, I totally understand," Hannah said. "Who wants to miss out on those?"

At least she hadn't asked what Sage was doing here. Sage was still working on an explanation for that.

To change the topic, she pointed to the display case. "Is that what you and Patrick are after? Cinnamon rolls? We still have plenty. Ms. Bea made an extra batch this afternoon for some reason."

"Let me have three, please, and three of those pretty cupcakes to go. The chocolate ones."

"Dessert tonight for the mayor?"

"Exactly. Ms. Bea is a better baker than I am any day of the week. Right, Patrick?"

The small boy now near drooling on the glass, nodded. "Uh-huh."

The two woman exchanged smiles as Sage sacked the order.

When Hannah had paid and was about to leave, white bag in hand, she said, "Good catching up with you today, Sage. Let's get together sometime. Social media is okay but in person is so much better."

Sage thought her heart would stop.

*Social media. Social media!*

She managed to agree and to offer a friendly goodbye, but all the while her mind was going nuts. She'd totally forgotten about her social media accounts. Anyone looking for her, and she had no doubt someone was, could likely trace her through social media.

Had she posted anything since her arrival in Sundown Valley? Had she remembered to turn off the location on her cell phone?

Another customer came and went. Then the after-school group arrived like a swarm of starving, buzzing locusts. Although desperate to delete those social media accounts, Sage was too busy until after closing time.

Insisting Ms. Bea go home at six, she stayed behind to clean and organize for tomorrow. With strict orders that they let Ms. Bea rest she allowed Ryder and Paisley to accompany the older woman.

As soon as they were out of sight, she yanked her phone from her pocket and deleted, deactivated and blocked everything she could think of, including turning off her phone's data.

Gnawing at her lip, she stared at the device. Had she done everything necessary to cover her tracks? She'd yet to contact Amy to let her know the kids were okay, but was doing so wise? Amy was in jail. Police listened in to prisoners' calls, didn't they?

What if she used the bakery phone? No. Not that. Anyone looking for her could easily discover she worked here.

Why were there so few pay phones left in this country?

If she had the extra money, she'd buy one of those untraceable burner phones like in cop movies.

"You're in deep thought."

Sage jumped. The cell phone clattered to the tile floor.

"Bowie!" Her heart stopped, started again and pounded like a teenager with a new drum set.

He'd startled her. Plain and simple. That's why her pulse jittered and sputtered.

But she *was* glad to see him.

Yesterday, she'd enjoyed church and the fellowship dinner afterward. People were friendly if curious and maybe even speculative when she'd arrived with Bowie.

Apparently, he didn't bring women his age to church very often.

She refused to think about what that might mean.

"Sorry." He scooped the cell phone from the tile, looked it over and returned it. "No harm done."

"Except to my heart." She pressed a hand over the left side of her baker's apron.

The spokes around his eyes creased in a smile. "Didn't mean to startle you." He jerked a thumb over one shoulder. "The front door was still unlocked."

She dropped her head back in aggravation. She'd been so distracted by the social media worry, she hadn't locked up. "Oh, good gravy, I forgot."

As she started that direction, sliding the cell phone into a pocket, he snagged her elbow. "I locked it."

"You have a key?"

"How else can I work on her Methuselah equipment at night?"

"Good point. But everything's working great right now."

"Nice to know. Got any leftover food? Wade and Kyra will be home tonight."

She rolled that around in her head and interpreted it to mean he wanted to provide a treat for the newlyweds when they arrived home. A welcome back. One of his good deeds for people he cared about. Which seemed to be everyone.

Her included.

Another reason not to read anything romantic into their weekend together.

"Ms. Bea would want you to have anything you wanted. She always makes extra that she gives away after closing. Look in the display case. I'll hand you a carry-out box."

"I wasn't asking for freebies."

"Too bad. You're getting them." She perched a hand on her hip and shot him a *so-there* look. "Ms. Bea already took the cash bag to the bank. No sales allowed."

He raised both hands in surrender. "I never argue over doughnuts."

"Or anything else."

"Only the important things." He took the offered box and filled it. "A lot of leftovers today."

"She overbakes on Monday."

"Ah, yes, her day to celebrate with townspeople."

"Uh-huh."

He paused, squinting at the display case in thought. "Do you have plans for the rest of these?"

"No. Why?"

He pointed a finger at her, eyes alight with enthusiasm. "Grab a couple of boxes. I have an idea."

She got the cartons and joined him in filling them. "Are you going to tell me what we're doing?"

"Police and fire." He added a final lemon cream doughnut, the only one of its kind that hadn't sold. "They work nights. Let's take them a treat."

*Police?* Sage's belly took a nose dive. Not a good plan. "You take them. I have too much to do here."

Closing the lid on the boxes, she patted the see-through tops and handed them over.

The animation left Bowie's face. She'd disappointed him.

She was sorry about that, but he'd be a lot more disappointed if she'd gone along and he had to watch her get arrested.

* * *

During the next week and a half, Bowie stole time here and there to work on his projects. With Wade back on the ranch, some of the pressure was off. Still, he was aware of every tick of the clock and each sunset moving him closer and closer to the deadline.

Three designs were complete, at least on paper, with two cut and one in the process of tooling.

Watching the scene come to life beneath his fingers thrilled him.

He talked to God as he worked, wondering out loud if this inner joy was anything close to the emotion God had felt when he created the universe. For Bowie, creating art was a spiritual endeavor that came from someplace deep inside him. A God thing.

In the distance, he heard a motor, recognizing the sound as Wade's truck.

He schooled himself for another interruption. Patience was a virtue he'd learned well while training horses.

When the exterior door scraped open and his cousin entered, Bowie put aside his round knife and turned toward his cousin.

Wade spoke first. "You're sure spending a lot of time out here lately. Christmas gifts?"

Bowie hitched a shoulder. "Maybe."

"Awesome." Wade didn't try to peek at the designs. "I was on my way to pasture 4 to put out protein tubs and saw your truck."

"You need my help?"

"I can handle it." He removed his hat, scrubbed the top of his head and put the black Stetson back on. "Anyway, Kyra and I dropped by the bakery while we were in town and invited them to dinner."

"You invited who to dinner?"

"Bea, Sage and her kids."

"Oh." Bowie's head bobbed. His pulse jolted. He'd managed to spend an entire week without giving in to the urge to see Sage. Telephone calls, sure, but no up close and personal temptation to kiss the daylights out of her.

"You don't seem enthused. Is there a problem?"

"Your house. Invite who you choose."

"I thought you liked her."

"I do."

Understanding dawned in Wade's eyes. "You still have a thing for her."

"Don't be ridiculous. I'm not that messed-up."

"What would be wrong with you and Sage getting together? You're both single, both Christians. Choices in this town are dwindling fast, old son."

"There's the problem. Sage won't be in this town that long."

"That a fact?"

"Those who don't remember history are doomed to repeat it. Like before, Sage has made it clear her stay in Sundown Valley is temporary."

"Sounds familiar."

Bowie waved him off. "Totally different situation than yours. Kyra was the staying kind. Sage is restless."

"Too bad. Nice girl. Kind of ugly, though." Then he laughed, joking as he turned to leave.

For the rest of his time in the shop, Bowie was hard-pressed to think of anything except the upcoming dinner with Sage and the kids.

Dinner at the Sundown Ranch with three toddlers was always a lively affair. Tonight, with the addition of Sage, Ryder and Paisley, minus Ms. Bea who needed to rest her "weary bones," the extended dining room table was full to overflowing.

In spite of his original misgivings, Bowie was enjoying himself.

He didn't see the point of fighting the inevitable when he could be having a good time. Sitting back in his chair, Bowie listened to the chatter with a grateful heart. God had given him so much. Family, friends, good food—three of the best things in life.

Why should he complain?

He wondered what Sage thought about all the noise and mess of the toddlers, what she thought of Wade's new wife, Kyra.

Red-haired Kyra with her perky smile and positive attitude was easy to like. She and Wade both had come home from Hawaii glowing with a joy Bowie tried not to envy. He was thrilled for them. But he wondered if he'd ever have that. Would he ever know what it was like to love and be loved in return?

"How was Hawaii?" Sage sat next to Bowie across the table from Kyra and Wade.

The newlyweds exchanged happy glances. Wade touched Kyra's nose. "Someone got a little too much sun."

Kyra's pink cheeks lifted. "Wade gets darker and I get pinker. Even with a hat and sunscreen."

Wade gave her a wink. "You look beautiful to me."

One of the triplets began to fuss. Kyra removed him from his high chair and stood him on the floor. "They're outgrowing these and a lot of other things. We need to get booster chairs and new clothes."

"Shopping!" Wade slapped his forehead in mock dismay.

"Did you see how short Ben's pants are now? And his shirt barely covers his belly."

"Thank goodness their beds convert into toddler beds."

Kyra bumped her shoulder against Wade's. "Wise purchase on your part, Daddy."

*Daddy.* Bowie got an empty, yearning tug in the pit of his stomach.

Love didn't envy. That was Bible. But it was hard not to want the kind of love and family his cousin had.

Abby, the miniature flirt, stretched her hands toward him. Bowie took her out of the high chair and held her on his lap. She reached for his Texas toast. He tore off a piece for her.

"Tank oo."

He melted. He gave her another piece.

"They're adorable babies," Sage said. She took Abby's little hand and shook it up and down. Abby offered her a bite of toast.

Sage chuckled, pushed back a strand of Abby's brown hair and pretended to take a bite. When Abby patted her cheek with a messy hand, Sage kissed it.

Kissed it, the way she'd kissed his palm the day they'd gone riding. A friendly little peck. Not a romantic moment.

Yet, the action turned his insides as soft and warm as homemade pudding.

Bowie accepted the truth that had bugged him since he'd first seen Sage in the Bea Sweet. He was falling in love with her again. Maybe he'd always loved her, though this was not the teenage crush of old, but something steady and long-lasting.

Anyway, it would last a long time for him.

Sage was the reason he'd never found the right woman. She was the reason he'd dragged his feet about moving out of the main house. The rudimentary plans for his own home had been in his possession for years. He hadn't built because he hadn't wanted to live alone.

He'd been waiting for something that wasn't likely to ever happen.

He needed to get on with life. Put Sage in her appropriate place and move on.

"I'm thinking about building a house," he blurted before his brain could stop his mouth.

Three sets of adult eyes turned his way.

"You've talked about doing that for years," Wade said.

"Maybe it's time."

"This is your home as much as mine."

That much was true. "You have a family now. This house should be yours and Kyra's alone."

Concern tugged Kyra's pale eyebrows together. "You aren't saying this because of me, are you? Because I've moved in?"

That was part of it. Hadn't he begun to feel like a third wheel? They didn't need him around.

"You *are* newlyweds."

His words made Kyra blush. "I won't be responsible for coming between you and Wade."

"You wouldn't be. Besides, right now, I'm just making conversation. I can't start building anytime soon." Not until he learned how lucrative the retail contracts would be. *If* he could make the deadline. *If* the board of JP Enterprises liked his work. If, if, if.

He offered Kyra a friendly wink. "Don't worry. You'll never get rid of me for good."

Kyra eased back in her chair, mollified.

Wade put his fork aside. "He can't go far. I need him. This ranch is as much his as mine."

Though he was confident and comfortable in his role as partner on the Sundown, Bowie had needed to hear that. He sometimes struggled with the fact that he was a cousin, not a brother like Yates, who didn't appreciate the gift he'd been given.

Bowie did.

But he also needed something that was his alone, something he'd earned for himself.

"Do you still want to build near your workshop overlooking the valley?" Wade asked.

"Yes."

"That's a great spot."

"It's gorgeous up there." Kyra began removing plastic dishes from the high chairs. "If I didn't love this place so much, I'd be jealous."

Bowie glanced to his side at Sage. She'd remained silent during the exchange. Building a house had probably never been on her radar.

He didn't really want to build a house and live in it alone. Not forever, like Jinx.

The idea of a future in an empty house stretched before him.

Maybe someday he'd be smart enough to fall in love with a woman who wanted to settle down. A woman who longed for home and family as much as he did. A woman who'd love him back.

# *Chapter Ten*

While the triplets, joined by Ryder and Paisley, played with a mountain of toys, the adults began a spirited game of Scrabble, laughing insanely when partners Wade and Bowie created ridiculous word forms such as *zuquij* and *xtrapulaz*.

"Zuquij is a disease of cattle. Right, Bowie?"

Keeping a straight face for his cousin's sake, Bowie rubbed his chin as if in deep thought. "Similar to xtrapulaz. Bad, very bad for cattle."

Kyra squinted one eye at her new husband. "Why am I having a hard time believing two Christian men?"

"Probably because they cheat." Sage pointed a brown game tile toward the two guys.

Wade pumped his eyebrows. "All's fair in love and Scrabble."

Bowie wished that was true. At least the love part.

When Sage gave him a mock glare, he jerked a thumb toward Wade. "What he said."

Everyone laughed.

In the end, the ladies won anyway and the men bemoaned their fate.

"Women really are smarter," Wade said.

"I already knew that," Bowie joked. He'd loved watching Sage chew at the side of her thumbnail, her face set in determined concentration as she moved tiles around.

Kyra had come up with a real word that sealed the deal. *Quixotic*. Then, to really drive the nail in the men's coffin, she joined it with two other words that blew the rest of them out of the water.

"This was such fun." Sage pushed back from the game table and stood. "Thank you for inviting me."

Bowie stood too. They all had to get up early. Him especially if he hoped to get a couple of hours in the workshop. "I'll walk you to your car."

"Ryder, Paisley," Sage said, "time to go."

Ryder let out a groan. Bowie considered this complaint a positive sign. Playing with the triplets and his sister relaxed the little worrywart, although he still wouldn't let Paisley out of his sight for a minute. He even guarded the bathroom door when she was inside.

As they walked out to the porch, talking, saying farewells and threatening to study the dictionary for the next Scrabble battle, Kyra lifted Caden into her arms and snuggled his neck.

"It's been great getting to know you better, Sage. Please come back anytime. You're always welcome."

"I'd like that."

Helplessly, Bowie admitted to himself, he would too. And then considered banging his head against the door facing.

Wade slipped an arm around his wife's waist and the couple turned back inside the house, shutting the door.

The porch light lit the way to the Jeep. Bowie walked along, dragging his feet a little, hesitant to end such an enjoyable night. Wishing he had better sense and accepting that maybe he didn't.

Oh, he would keep fighting it. He had to.

Had he developed some psychological compulsion to care about people he knew would inevitably leave him?

The thought was worth pondering.

Sage opened the back passenger door. When she

reached for Paisley, the child turned big eyes on Bowie and lifted her arms.

A rush of pleasure spread through Bowie. The little girl, both the kids to be honest, had wormed their way into his affections. They needed him. He liked the feeling.

Sage widened her eyes as if to say, "What's that about?"

Stepping around Sage, he lifted the little girl into his arms. She weighed about as much as a kitten. As he settled her in the child safety seat, Paisley clung to his neck a moment longer than necessary.

In the dome light, he brushed her baby-fine hair away from her face and smiled into her eyes. Smiling softly in return, she touched his cheek with her tiny fingers.

He wondered if this was what it felt like to be a father.

Ryder had climbed in on the other side and scooted close as if to protect his sister.

Bowie ruffled the boy's hair. "Good night, bud."

He closed the door and turned to find Sage leaning her back against the driver's door, watching him.

He got a funny feeling, knowing her full attention was on him.

"He had fun. We all did." Dangly silver earrings with small teardrop ends caught the light and twinkled like stars against her dark hair. "I really like Kyra, and Wade is great. He's so different now."

"Maturity does that to some people."

"You've always been an old soul, haven't you?"

Which meant he'd been boring in high school. Was he still?

"I guess." Living on the streets would definitely age a child.

"I never saw Wade as the settling down type."

"No? I did. He sowed some wild oats, but he has this land and ranching in his blood."

"He's good with those babies." She bumped him with a shoulder. "So are you."

"They're fun. But when they cry, I hand them over."

She scoffed. "You'd make a great dad."

"Not in the market."

"And why is that? You're planning to build a house in the near future. Which by the way, I want to see those plans." She poked a finger into his biceps.

He rubbed the spot, pretending injury.

Snickering, she said, "You deserve to find a girl as nice as you are, get married, and fill that new house with family."

Deserve? He'd been given so much. He didn't believe he deserved anything.

Besides, his heart had already closed up shop. He didn't tell her that.

What was the use?

As the days passed, Sage began to relax. The town was friendly. No one was suspicious. Fact was they welcomed her like a long-lost friend.

Even the social media scare had come to nothing.

She was beginning to think she was safe.

Part of that was due to Bowie. The man wore an aura of safety, as if the world could run to him, and he'd protect it.

He seemed to always be there when she needed him. Not just her, but any number of people in town. They called. He came to the rescue.

Her best friend from high school was even better as an adult. Yes, they spent a lot of time together. At the ranch, in the bakery, at Ms. Bea's house, at church. That's what friends did.

She'd even grown accustomed to taking leftover sweets to the police department, some of which she'd baked herself.

Working side by side with Ms. Bea, she'd learned a

considerable amount about baking. To her utter shock, she enjoyed it. Like Bea, she found pleasure in the people, the community, the daily ebb and flow of life in a small town.

It was healing. *She* was healing. Some days she thought Ryder was better too, though Paisley was still too fearful to speak to anyone but him.

She didn't know what else to do to help Amy's children. She was praying. So were Bea and Bowie.

Bowie dropped by a couple of times a week, more when something broke down, and they invariably ended up making plans together. She didn't know who instigated the invitations, her or him, but she and the kids liked spending time with the rancher.

They'd gone for a burger, to Bible study, church outings, a bonfire before the homecoming football game.

Good times.

She wanted to believe that their relationship was the same as it had been in high school. Best buds.

It couldn't be anything more.

If her heart beat a little faster and joy bubbled up in her chest anytime he walked into the bakery, she ignored it.

She could not fall in love with anyone. Certainly not Bowie. She never wanted to cause him grief.

Though unsure of how deep his feelings for her went, she knew he cared, especially for the kids. After learning about the New Orleans shelter he supported, she realized that kids were his passion. His ministry, he claimed. All kids, not just her niece and nephew.

Pushing him away now was the wiser, kinder thing to do. And yet, she could not bring herself to be without him.

Most nights after closing, she called him. Sometimes he was distracted, working on something in his shop. Secrets, he claimed, and she suspected he was creating Christmas presents for her and the kids. Yet, for all his busyness, he always came if she asked, and they'd sit awhile on Ms. Bea's porch swing, listening to the night.

Bowie wasn't a talker, but Sage was, and he let her talk all she wanted.

Naturally, she avoided the big issue, the one that threatened to destroy her tiny haven of safety and shatter their friendship for good.

Bowie stepped back from the workbench to gaze at the completed piece of handcrafted, perfectly tooled and burnished leather. He liked it, was proud of it, could almost imagine it dangling from a woman's shoulder. The problem was, this was only the first of many yet to do, and the days were sweeping past.

Taking the bag to a cabinet he'd prepared for this project, he hung it inside. Last night, he'd cut out another and was ready to sketch designs for still more. Ready, but not there yet.

His cell phone jangled.

One glance identified the caller as Katherine Pembroke.

"Hello. Bowie here."

"Bowie. Katherine Pembroke." Her no-nonsense tone straightened his spine. "We have a bit of a problem."

The straight spine stiffened into a two-by-four. "Oh?"

"One of my board members must be out of the country on December 21. With that in mind we need to move up our due date."

He wanted to protest, to remind her that they had a contract, but if he did, he stood a good chance of making her angry enough to reject his work outright. The option was hers. She held the cards.

"What do you have in mind?"

"I know it's added pressure, but Geoffrey is leaving on the 17. Can you get the items to me by December 16?"

Nearly a week early? Was she serious?

"I'm an artist, Ms. Pembroke. Art takes time to perfect."

"Understandable. I know the artistic temperament. Need I reminder you, however, that this is a chance many leather crafters would do anything to get?"

"No, ma'am. I'll figure something out."

"Excellent. Talk soon."

The phone clicked in his ear. He stared at the device for ten long seconds. Then he pocketed the phone and sorted through his designs, looking at the pieces he'd begun.

He was in trouble. More importantly, Isaiah House was in need. Kids' lives were at risk.

He could do this. He had to.

Somehow.

The call from Principal Feldman came in just after two o'clock. Ryder and Paisley were gone.

"Gone?" Sage clutched the bakery landline receiver to her ear. Her brain went wild. Her mouth went dry. "How could they be gone?"

They'd been at school, surrounded by adults.

Had they been kidnapped? Had Amy somehow escaped jail and stolen her own kids?

A shot of fear stopped Sage's heart. Had social services learned of their situation and taken them?

No, that didn't make sense. The school would have been informed if social services was involved.

These things raced through her mind so fast, Mr. Feldman's words barely broke through the panic. "Ryder got in a fight with Owen on the playground at recess. We think he may have run away and taken Paisley with him."

Run away. "I don't understand. How could that be possible? Where were the teachers?"

"We don't know but rest assured I am looking into it. I was hoping they were there with you."

"I haven't seen him. Maybe he went to the house, instead of coming to the bakery. I'll go there and call you back."

"If he isn't at home, I'll alert the police to be on the lookout."

"Don't do that," she said quickly. "Not yet. Let us look for him. I—I might know where he is."

Not really, but she knew some places to look.

On the other end of the line, Mr. Feldman hesitated, but finally agreed. "All right. Keep me posted."

A moment of relief that the police wouldn't be involved was replaced by worry. Where were Ryder and Paisley?

She'd relaxed a little, had let her guard down and now this.

Without a moment's thought, she dialed Bowie's number.

When he answered, she blurted, "Ryder's run away."

"Paisley with him?"

"Yes."

She could hear him moving, hear keys rattle. "I'm on my way."

By the time Bowie drove the ten miles from the ranch into town, Sage had scoured the streets between the bakery and Bea's house, hoping to spy a small, orange-shirted boy and a tiny girl with red bows in her hair.

Once inside the rambling two-story, she ran from room to room, calling out, looking under beds, inside closets and behind anything with space.

A car door slammed and she rushed to the front of the house as her favorite rancher stormed up the walkway like a soldier on a mission.

Pushing the screen door with the flat of her hand, Sage rushed out to meet him.

*Bowie was here.*

She fell against his strong chest. His muscled arms came around her, holding her lightly to him.

"It'll be okay. We'll find them."

His calm, confident manner eased the fear growing in her like a cancer. They had to find the kids and find them fast. Losing Amy's children twice could cause trouble she was not ready to face.

She nodded. Her cheek brushed the soft cotton of his maroon shirt. Beneath her ear, she felt the steady, reassuring beat of his heart.

Somehow being in Bowie's arms made everything better. She didn't want to move, didn't want to leave the safe refuge he always provided.

Reluctantly, she eased back, hands resting lightly at his waist.

"What happened?" Bowie asked. "Why did he run away?"

"He got in a fight on the playground. I don't have details."

"He may be hiding somewhere in the school."

"They're looking, but whatever happened on the playground set off his protective instincts. He has Paisley with him, which means he's probably left the school grounds. He still talks about seeing Amy and may believe he can walk to Kansas City."

"You think so?"

"I don't know what to think. He was doing so much better. I hadn't heard a hint of trouble. He didn't like getting out of bed in the mornings, but he seemed to look forward to seeing his new friends every day."

"Then hold to the positive thoughts. He's better off here in Sundown Valley than he was before, and he knows it."

She couldn't argue with a man who'd been in Ryder's shoes. "I hope so. I'm heading to the park for a look. He and Paisley like the wooden fort."

"Good idea. I'll drive to the gravel pit. It's not that far from the school."

"Okay." The gravel pit had become a favorite hangout of exploring kids and romantic teens. She hoped he hadn't gone there. "He's fascinated by big equipment."

Dangerous equipment.

"Lots of hidey holes out there."

An hour and a dozen text messages later, they met back at the house, empty-handed.

At Bowie's request, Sage searched the house again, upstairs and down. The kids' clothes and toys were exactly where they'd left them.

She stepped out on the back porch. Bea's chickens clucked at her. Could the kids be inside the chicken house?

"Bowie." She pointed.

He nodded and without a word, went inside the pen, bending his tall frame to the short opening of the coop door.

Sage held her breath. When Bowie straightened and shook his head, she wilted, her breath coming out in a disappointed gust.

"Not under the porch either. I looked." He exited the pen, walked to the fence bordering the alley and gazed up in the huge pecan tree hanging over the back yard.

Crepe myrtles bordered each side of the back porch, too small for hideaways.

Standing in the middle of the yard, Bowie turned in a slow circle. Suddenly, he stopped. His eyes locked on hers.

"Have you looked in the garage?"

"Yes. The storage shed too."

"The storm shelter?"

Years ago, Ron and Bea had installed a shelter in the floor of the garage. "Paisley's afraid of the dark."

"Ryder has a flashlight. I gave it to him."

They raced each other to the garage. She was a runner with a head start. He was in cowboy boots. She won. A close second, he reached around her and yanked open the metal door.

"Ryder?" Bowie's voice was as calm and easy as if he

was rocking a baby. No fear-inducing panic. "Buddy, are you down there?"

Ducking his head, the big man trotted down the steps, his boots clicking on the concrete. Sage was right behind him.

No light. No sound.

Her hope dwindled.

Requiring a moment for her eyes to adjust to the dim confines, Sage paused at the bottom of the steps. The interior was small but big enough to squeeze in six or eight people to shelter from a tornado.

Then she heard the sweetest sound.

"You're safe, buddy. Paisley's safe too."

She rounded the corner of the doorway to see Bowie squatting in front of the two children. They crowded together in one shadowed corner. Paisley clutched her brother and her lovey. Ryder clutched a flashlight. He must have heard them and turned off the light. Bowie clicked it on.

Sage sat down on the concrete bench next to Paisley and put an arm around her. The little girl leaned her head on Sage, sighing as if relieved to be found.

"Want to tell us what happened?" Bowie asked. "Why you ran away?"

"We didn't run away. We just came home."

Home. That he viewed this big old house as home was progress.

Softly, she asked, "Why did you come home?"

Ryder shrugged, his expression closing up as he stared at the wall.

Bowie put his wide hands on each of Ryder's knees, light and easy, but enveloping the small bones. "The principal said you had a fight."

The boy remained silent.

"Help us understand, Ryder," Sage said. "Why did you hit Owen?"

"He's mean."

"Did he do something to you first?"

Ryder's eyes cut to his sister. Suspicion sprouted in Sage.

"Was this about Paisley?"

"He said she was stupid because she wouldn't talk to him. He called her names. The other kids laughed and made her cry. I hate them."

"Taking up for your sister is a heroic thing to do." Bowie stretched to a stand, stooped beneath the low roof. "Did you tell this to Mr. Feldman?"

"No."

"Want me to talk to him?"

Ryder looked up at the cowboy as if he couldn't believe anyone would take his side. "Am I in trouble?"

"Fighting is against the rules. Bullying preschool students is also against the rules." Sage stood and reached for Paisley's hand. "We'll get this straightened out."

"Fairly," Bowie said. "You have my word on that."

"A man's only as good as his word, right?"

Ryder's question would have been cute if it hadn't been so heartrending.

Serious as could be, Bowie nodded. "Right."

"Come on." Sage pulled Paisley to her feet. "I need a snack. How about you?"

As though the weight of the world had left his shoulders, Ryder followed the others out of the shelter.

The children were safe for now. They were all safe, thanks to Bowie.

How long before something else happened and this little cocoon she'd let Bowie build around them fell apart?

Even Bowie couldn't save her from herself.

Sage insisted Bowie stay for dinner. After today, she owed him that much.

At first, he'd begged off, citing work still to be done in

his shop. But when Ryder had chimed in, pleading for him to stay a little bit longer, he'd capitulated. The man was a pushover where these kids were concerned.

Afterward, Bowie and Ryder practiced addition facts while she and Paisley worked a jigsaw puzzle of the alphabet.

It was a family kind of scene. And she realized having Bowie near mattered more to her than she should allow.

Ms. Bea arrived home from the bakery and ate dinner before retiring to her room. Her limp was worse tonight and she moved slower than before, a result of not having Sage's help this afternoon.

A shaft of guilt shot through Sage, followed by a worry. How would Ms. Bea manage when she was no longer in town?

The family feeling lingered as Bowie helped her get the kids into bed. Tucking a soft blanket beneath Paisley's chin, she whispered a prayer over the child before kissing the clean-scented forehead. Paisley's thin arms snaked around her neck and squeezed.

Throat clogged with emotion, Sage left the nightlight burning and crossed the hall to Ryder's room.

Bowie sat on the side of the twin bed, talking softly to the boy as he tugged the covers to his neck.

When he saw Sage standing in the doorway, Bowie rose and gently ruffled Ryder's damp hair. "Night, bud."

Ryder gripped the edge of his blanket. His knuckles were pale. "Are you coming over tomorrow night?"

"You want me to?"

"Yeah." Ryder dropped his gaze, fiddling with the blanket's binding. "You don't have to if you're busy."

"A man is never too busy for a friend."

That was Bowie. Anything for a friend.

Satisfied, Ryder sank deeper into his pillow.

Leaving the light on, the adults stepped into the hallway.

"Does he ever feel secure?" she murmured, aching with love and sick to know her sister had neglected her son's emotional security.

"No. He doesn't," Bowie said. "Not yet anyway."

She reached for Bowie's hand, gazing down at the long, hardworking fingers of a man who'd also suffered through a rocky childhood. "I see the way you relate to him. And him to you."

He didn't answer.

"Can he heal?"

"With God all things are possible. That's not a platitude." He laced his fingers with hers. "God put you in their lives. That means something, I think."

Sage hoped so. She really hoped so.

She rubbed the back of a tight, tired neck. If she didn't relax awhile, she'd never sleep. "How about some cocoa?"

Having Bowie around eased her. It was as if he could make everything turn out all right. She definitely wasn't ready for him to go home.

His dark eyebrows lifted. Humor sparkled in those dark chocolate eyes. "With marshmallows?"

"Loads and tons."

His mouth twitched. "Must be some seriously large mugs."

A sensible woman would grab onto a man like Bowie and never let go.

Except she couldn't.

Adjourning to the eat-in kitchen, they shared cocoa and conversation. She talked. As usual, Bowie added a word or two to keep things moving.

"How are your house plans coming along?" she asked at one point. "You never did show them to me."

"I will."

"When?"

"Anytime you want. They're in the truck."

She whacked his forearm. “Get them! I want to see.”

Chuckling, he did as she asked, returning with a long, wide roll of paper.

As he spread the hand-sketched plans on the table, he said, “I’m still making changes, tweaking things. It’s nowhere near ready for the architect.”

“Planning a house is fun.” She rubbed her hands together in anticipation. “I’ve watched HGTV.”

“Which makes you an expert.” His eyes twinkled. “I need your opinions.”

“Oh, I have plenty of those.”

Bowie laughed. He enjoyed being with Sage, even if he’d regret it later when he had to stay up half the night in his workshop.

Like a bomb threatening to go off, time slipped away from him. He was down to a few weeks to finish the work. Katherine Pembroke’s phone call had been a reminder to step up his pace. Somehow.

That Sage, the woman he thought about far more than fancy leather, was interested in his house plans flattered him. Might as well get her input. Women viewed a home differently than men. At least, he thought they did.

He’d done absolutely nothing on the house plans or the building site since making his grand announcement at Wade’s dinner table. It could be years before he built this house, and now, he wished he’d said nothing at all.

Sage moved up next to where he bent over the table. Bowie caught the subtle scent of baby shampoo and something indefinably Sage. Earthy, warm, feminine.

His stomach jittered. He fought the feeling, though it was useless. He loved her all over again. Maybe more than ever. Being with her was right in so many ways.

And wrong in so many others.

As he pointed to the home’s layout, she tapped the upstairs dormers. "I love those on a house. They're so homey. Like a place of refuge and security, filled with happy family."

Was that what she longed for? A place of refuge? Security? Were those the things she searched for in her restless moves from town to town?

He cleared his throat and tried not to think about any of those things. He could fix an oven or a car. He couldn't fix Sage's restless heart, no matter how much he wanted to.

"What about the kitchen design? Do you like an open floor plan like this or the rooms more segmented?"

"Open, definitely." She slid a purple fingernail from the kitchen island to the great room. "Sight lines to everywhere."

"That's what Kyra said. She likes being able to see the triplets from anywhere in the living space."

Sage swung her focus from the sketches to him. The long hair she'd loosened from a ponytail hours ago swept against his shoulder.

"These plans are for a big house, Bowie. Four bedrooms, two and half baths, a game room and a huge living area. This is a family home, not a bachelor pad."

The jittery gut came again.

"Yeah, well," he shrugged, "a man can always hope."

She went still, her green gaze lasered into him as if she saw his deepest secrets. He sure hoped not.

"What is it that you hope for, Bowie?"

*You.* A half dozen kids—bio, foster, adopted, he didn't care.

But he said, "I have everything a man could want except my own family, I suppose. Not that I'm complaining. My life is good. But I don't want to be a bachelor forever."

Not like Jinx, alone with only his Irish setter. And now the four puppies she'd had.

Sure, Bowie would always have his cousins. They were

partners, nearly brothers. Even if Yates never came home again, Bowie had Wade and the triplets and now Kyra, which may have been the cause for his sudden need to create his own space in the world.

The recent wedding and forever stuff had wiggled its way into his head.

Sage nodded slowly, those Mountain Dew eyes still holding him. "I can see you married, with a family. You're such a stable guy and great with kids. You're the marrying kind, Bowie Trudeau."

His heart set up a thundering pace, squeezing with a hope he quickly repressed. "What about you, Sage? Can you see yourself married with kids? Are you the marrying kind?"

She dropped her attention to the sprawling home he wanted to build someday, quiet for long, aching moments in which he wished he hadn't asked.

"Someday. Maybe. When I'm ready to grow roots. When the right man comes along."

And there he had his answer.

# *Chapter Eleven*

Bad things came in threes. Sage had always heard that and decided it was true.

Why didn't *good* things come in threes? Or even twos? Why was it always the bad stuff?

As she stood at Ms. Bea's side inside the Sundown Valley Physicians Clinic, these thoughts raced through her mind. Unwanted. Persistent. Like a stomach virus through an elementary school.

Bad things come in threes. Was this the second or the third?

She'd only been absent from the bakery long enough to take the kids to school.

She'd returned to find Bea on the kitchen floor, covered in flour with a half-dozen customers gathered around as if she were dead. The baker had slipped and fallen, twisted her arm and ankle and banged her head against the rolling bakery rack.

At Bea's insistence, they had not called an ambulance which would have taken too long to get there anyway. Two firefighters, at the bakery for hot doughnuts, had formed a human gurney and carried her to a waiting car.

"Much ado about nothing," Bea fussed from her perch on a slick vinyl exam table. She clutched an ice pack to the back of her head. Two more draped across her ankle and opposite wrist. "I'm more embarrassed than injured."

"Ms. Bea, you're hurt. You couldn't put enough weight on your left leg to get off the floor by yourself."

"Which is not the least bit abnormal for someone my age."

Sage could argue that point but she didn't. Debilitating arthritis was not normal.

"You may have a concussion. Marty Westheimer said you were unconscious for a minute or two."

"Was I?" Bea blinked, troubled. "No wonder I have a headache."

"Let's see what the doctor has to say."

"Did you lock the bakery before you left?" Before Sage could nod, Bea went on. "I hate to think of all the people who won't have breakfast this morning."

"There are other places in Sundown Valley to eat."

Bea's eyes flared. "You hush your mouth."

The comment was only half jest. Sage snickered anyway.

"You're right. Sundown Valley loves the bakery and you. The shop is an important community gathering spot, but for this one day, people will have to manage. They'll appreciate you and the bakery more after today."

"I don't know what would happen if I had to close for very long."

The bakery was Ms. Bea's baby, and the town was the children she'd never had. Yet, the time was coming when she could not manage a full-time bakery alone.

Neither of them wanted to think about that.

"Don't borrow trouble. Wasn't that what you always told me? Let's wait for the X-ray results."

Bea grabbed her hand. "If the news is bad, will you take over the bakery until I get back on my feet?"

Take over? How could she? For how long?

The notion of agreeing to anything long-term frightened her. What if someone came looking for Ryder and Paisley? What if she had to leave unexpectedly?

Praying for direction, aware of how much she owed Bea Cunningham, she said the only thing she could.

"Of course I will."

And she'd pray every day that she could keep that promise.

* * *

The verdict was in. Ms. Bea had pulled back muscles, a sprained ankle, a hairline fracture in her wrist, a mild concussion and a bruised hip.

She would heal. Eventually. The doctor ordered her to stay home and take it easy for at least a week and then report back to him.

Bea wasn't happy but she agreed to follow orders. For now.

Which meant Sage had a promise to keep. She was now in charge of the Bea Sweet Bakery.

In her time in Sundown Valley, she'd learned a lot from Ms. Bea about running the small hometown business, but not nearly enough. She could handle the sales and the cleaning and the packaged items. She could also bake simple items and fry doughnuts, though Ms. Bea's weekly treats and fancy breads were out of the question.

For the next week, the menu chalkboard would feature far fewer offerings.

By six the next morning, the bakery was open for business again. Hannah Redding had offered to take the children to school and Ms. Bea's next-door neighbor promised to look in on Bea every few hours.

Sage had risen early enough to organize a comfy chair in front of the TV surrounded by plenty of drinks, snacks, books and crochet yarn. Even the kids got in on the pampering, bringing pillows to prop Bea's leg and a throw blanket for her lap.

With a shy smile, Paisley had left a coloring book and crayons nearby.

Bea had fussed, embarrassed to be "helpless," but Sage could tell she was touched.

Rubbing her hands down the sides of a white apron, Sage unlocked the entrance to the Bea Sweet Bakery and flipped over the open sign. She took a deep breath. She could do this. She had to.

She was a nervous wreck.

With flour and sugar flying and doughnuts frying, she rushed from the kitchen to the eating area, filling the cases, making coffee, setting up for the morning rush.

When it hit, she became a whirlwind, running from one thing to the next, sacking doughnuts, topping coffee cups, icing Long Johns. The morning became a blur.

Everyone wanted to know how Ms. Bea was doing. They wanted details. She didn't have time for details.

Tension built in her shoulders and neck. She couldn't fail. She couldn't.

How had Ms. Bea done this alone?

By midmorning, she was exhausted. Frazzled. She'd never understood the meaning of the word before. Now, she did.

Frazzled was feeling like all the threads that held her together had come loose and were sticking out in every direction, flapping in the breeze she created by racing from chore to chore.

"Bea's sore but the doctor says she'll heal," she said for what must have been the hundredth time that morning.

She rang up the woman's bag of sugared doughnut holes and two coffees. "Thank you. I'll tell her you asked."

The jaunty little bell over the door jingled. More customers flooded in.

The preacher and one of the deacons abandoned their usual table and exited the store. Pastor Blake had promised to pay Bea a visit. Someone grabbed his table before Sage could wipe it down.

The oven beeped. She hustled back to the kitchen in time to save a batch of muffins.

She yanked the tray out of the stove. The heat came right through the potholder. She lost her grip.

The muffins clattered to the floor and went flying in all directions.

Fighting panic and the urge to run out the back door and not return, she stared in silent frustration at the spilled food.

The bell over the entrance jingled. Normally, a friendly hello, this morning the sound pushed her over the brink.

Collapsing at the bistro table to catch her breath and wonder what had made her think she could run a bakery, she thrust her head into her hands.

Heat and the smell of hot wasted banana muffins floated around her.

They were her favorite. She'd baked them herself. With crunchy streusel. She was so proud of them.

Now they were ruined.

Two boot toes appeared in her line of vision. Something that felt like the first winds of relief whispered in her ear. She recognized those boots.

Bowie went to his haunches in front of her. His hands rested on her knees. Just that connection reminded her that she was not alone. She had been, but she wasn't now.

He already knew about Ms. Bea. She'd called him with the news. He'd been in the middle of a difficult calving, but he'd promised to come into town to see the patient as soon as he could.

"Hey, pretty girl. You okay?"

She moaned. "I'm having a pity party."

He didn't laugh or scold. Bless him. He just waited.

"I let Ms. Bea down. This one little thing she asked of me, and I'm failing."

He nudged her chin upward. Her hands fell to her sides. He must think her the biggest whiner on the planet. Normally strong, tough and resilient, today she felt as limp and useless as the smashed bananas inside those ruined muffins.

"I want to do this, Bowie," she said. "I *need* to. I *owe* her."

"Ms. Bea doesn't expect perfection, you know. She does what she does out of love. You don't have to earn it."

She paused to gaze at him, curious, touched. "You know how I feel, don't you?"

Something shifted over his face. "I know."

Was this how he'd felt about his aunt and uncle? That he needed to repay them for taking him in as a son and an heir? To earn their kindness?

The insight into the man moved her. She was very tempted to touch his cheek, which was so ridiculous she knew she must really be frazzled.

He patted the top of her knee. "I'm here now. We'll get this done together."

"I can't ask you to do that. You have your own work."

He gazed around the kitchen, a soft smile tilting his lips. "I always wanted to work in a bakery."

Sage couldn't hold back a snort. "Liar."

He winked. "Let's go get 'em, tiger. We got this."

As usual, Bowie arrived and the world righted itself on its axis. Her world anyway.

Some woman, someday, was going to be very, very blessed to have this fine cowboy as a life partner.

Try as she might, she couldn't help being jealous of that woman.

Bowie worked the front and left the kitchen area for Sage. She could bake and do the fancy decorating stuff. He could wipe down tables and ring up customers.

Texting Wade to let him know where he was, he received a reply. You're hopeless. I don't know why you don't do something about her.

Bowie didn't respond. No point. He and his cousin were like brothers. They practically read each other's minds.

Except Wade didn't understand everything. Sage viewed him as her BFF. Crossing that line into romance might cost him her friendship. Worse, it might be the impetus that sent her running away again.

He wasn't ready for her to leave Sundown Valley.

Though the pair of them were not as smooth and efficient as Ms. Bea, he and Sage worked compatibly together. The work got done. The bakery survived the day.

Plus, he made Sage laugh more than once, which made it worth losing an entire day of ranch and art work.

As they closed that evening, she filled him in on Ms. Bea's condition as of their last text message. A neighbor had spent most of the day with her. Another had brought them both lunch and cared for Ms. Bea's chickens. The church ladies were gearing up to visit.

The blessings of small-town living.

He told her about his conversation with the principal concerning Ryder's fight and the other boy's treatment of Paisley.

"Ryder gets one day of recess detention. Owen loses a week of recess and spends that time volunteering in the special needs classroom."

"Special needs. That's brilliant. Was it your idea?"

"Maybe."

She bumped him with her hip. "Don't be so modest. You're such a good peacemaker."

He followed her into the kitchen with two empty pastry trays.

"I have an idea."

"Already boxed and ready."

"What?" He blinked, uncomprehending.

"The leftovers. I'll take them by the police station." She motioned toward two white boxes. "Although there aren't as many tonight."

"Great. But I'm talking about Ryder."

"Ah." She plunged her hands into the hot, soapy sink water and came out with a wet cloth.

He set the trays aside and took the bleach-scented cloth from her and got busy wiping down counters and tables.

"Mark, the principal, says Ryder is still obsessed with worry about Paisley. Won't leave her side at lunch or on the playground. Asks to visit her classroom several times a day."

"His teacher told me. I've discussed it with him, promised she would be okay, but he can't seem to let go. I wish I knew why he thinks he has to be her guard dog." She lifted a shoulder and scratched at her nose. "I've asked. He won't tell me."

"Mark and the school counselor think they should be separated more often, not less. When Ryder discovers his sister is okay without him, maybe he'll loosen up."

Sage swiveled her head in his direction. A frown tugged at her eyebrows. "I don't know about that. Wouldn't he get more upset?"

He raised one finger. "Hear me out."

Nodding, she scrubbed at the trays and utensils he'd dumped in the water. "Okay. I'm listening. Not that I'll agree, but I'll listen."

Bowie put the cleaning cloth on the counter, one hand resting on it while he talked.

He didn't have time for this or for Ryder either, but he'd figure out something.

"Ryder's comfortable with me and he was real interested in my leatherwork."

"That's true. He talks about you and the ranch a lot. You've connected with him."

Bowie thought so too. They shared a kinship, a bond that only street kids would understand. Sage and Amy had been foster kids, but they'd never lived on the streets.

"What if I take him to the ranch on Saturday? Let him help me in the workshop instead of hanging around here. Give him a chance to be a kid without hovering over his sister every minute."

Leather craft was something he could do with the boy while still moving forward on his own projects.

Sage went still. Bowie figured she was about to shoot him down. Fine. She was the guardian, not him. "It's just an idea."

Slowly, she wiped her hands on a towel and turned to stare at him.

"Bowie Trudeau, you are the most amazing, most thoughtful, generous man. I could just kiss you."

His heart dropped to his knees, lay there panting and then soared back into this chest.

He gazed at her full, beautiful mouth, thought of all the times he'd been tempted and finally said, "I don't think I'd mind that one bit."

With the strangest expression flashing in her light eyes, she walked right up to him, put one hand on his thundering heart and another on the side of his face, and kissed him.

Warm from the dish water, her hands heated his chest, his cheek, his heart.

He couldn't help himself. He'd waited so long for this moment. His arms went around her as if they knew the way and he snugged her closer, letting his lips say all the things he'd never been able to voice.

He really shouldn't be doing this.

A surprised gasp escaped Sage, but she didn't back away. Instead, her arms went around his neck and he was absolutely positive she was kissing him with the same amount of fervor.

That was all it took. He was lost.

He slid one hand along the side of her soft cheek and into her hair. She had the heaviest, silkiest hair.

Bowie forgot where he was. Forgot about the bakery and the dirty tables waiting to be cleaned. Forgot about the contract deadline looming like a storm cloud.

Today's work, both here and at the ranch, remained on the periphery. None of it mattered.

He even ignored the little voice in the back of his head that had been warning against this moment for weeks.

The lingering aroma of baked sweets floated around them, pleasant and warm, but the flavor of Sage's mouth on his was pure intoxication.

If he was dreaming, he never wanted to wake up.

The kiss lingered, delicious and fulfilling. Bowie thought his heart might explode with happiness.

Then, as suddenly as it began, the kiss ended.

Sage loosened her grip and slowly eased back. She stared at him as if he was a stranger. She looked bemused, bewildered.

With an awkward laugh, she stepped away, turning her head, avoiding his gaze.

*Don't do that. Please don't do that,* he thought.

"Sage," he began. He started to reach for her, then let his hands drop.

She refused to look at him. "I'm sorry. I didn't mean to lose control like that. I was just…so…grateful for what you're doing with Ryder."

*Grateful?*

If that didn't bust a man's balloon and leave him holding the empty string, nothing would.

Silence reigned in the kitchen for several long, uncomfortable minutes.

Sage rattled dishes in the sink, her back turned to him.

What was left of his pride fell on the floor like the earlier muffins and died a terrible death.

Kissing her had been the best experience of his life.

But she called it gratitude.

He took the cleaning cloth and headed into the dining room.

That night, Sage sat at the upstairs window in her room at Bea's house, staring out at the neighborhood and the lights of the little town. She was tired, but she was also exhilarated in the strangest way.

Something strangely electric and beautiful had happened when she'd kissed Bowie. And he'd kissed her back.

In her messy life, she'd kissed plenty of men. Some had been awful. Some enjoyable. All forgettable.

Nothing, *nothing* compared to that moment when the nicest guy on the planet had touched his lips to hers. She'd felt his soft breath against her cheek, his tender embrace as if she was something precious, and most of all an intensity she'd never expected from quiet Bowie.

The man had a great mouth and knew how to use it.

It wasn't just that. Any man could learn fancy technique. She'd felt his heart in that kiss and in the way he'd gently caressed her face and stroked her hair.

And that troubled her.

Placing a palm against the cool window, she watched the lights go out in the houses on the street. The neighborhood was dark enough that she could see the moon and a few bright stars.

God was watching. She felt His presence, though she wished she understood Him better. Like Bowie, He didn't say a lot.

She reached for the Bible she kept on the nightstand. Sometimes she forgot to read it, but last week at church the pastor mentioned that God speaks through his Word, the Bible.

Would He speak to her?

Randomly she flipped through the slim volume, pausing at 1 Corinthians 13. Though she'd heard the love chapter read at weddings, she'd not given it much thought. Tonight, one phrase seemed to stand out.

"Seeketh not her own."

She read the phrase over and over, rewording it for clarity.

Closing the book, she replaced it on the nightstand and returned to the window, looking out as if she hoped to see God Himself standing on the grass below.

"Love doesn't think about itself, or consider its own needs and wants, but those of others. Is that what you're trying to tell me, Lord?"

And there she had her answer.

No matter how wonderful being more than a friend to Bowie was starting to sound, she had to consider his needs before hers. With a double secret hanging over her head, clogging her throat with panic every time she thought about drug addicts and Amy's kids, she couldn't let herself love him. Couldn't let him love her.

Not after she'd read this verse. She couldn't be selfish.

Forehead pressed against the cool glass, heart aching, she began to pray.

She prayed for the kids, for Amy, for Ms. Bea and the bakery. Then she prayed that nothing she had to do would hurt the finest man she'd ever known.

Bowie spread the burnished brown leather across his work space, eyeing the intricate custom design he'd begun late last night. Soon, if all went well and he wasn't interrupted a hundred times, the leather would become another, uniquely beautiful, custom-made handbag fit for the rich and famous.

He rolled his head in slow circles, listening to his neck pop.

He was tired to the bone.

Tired and worried.

He'd overextended himself. Time was running out to produce the kind of exclusive product PJ Enterprises required of him. Barely a month was left. He felt the tension of that looming date in his shoulders and hands, hands he needed for precise work.

If he failed, he'd lose his shot at seeing his art appreciated by someone other than his friends. He'd also lose a boatload of money.

Failure meant he couldn't send a fat check to the street shelter or begin building a house. Not for a long time.

The house didn't matter so much, but the shelter could mean life or death for kids on the streets.

Yet how was a man supposed to say no to his friends when they needed him?

Right now, Bea and Sage needed him.

When had he ever said no to Sage Walker?

At the bakery the next day, something amazing occurred. Sage still could barely take it in.

What happened was truly an answer to prayer.

A group of volunteers, properly vetted and organized by Pastor Cloud, took shifts helping Sage run the bakery.

"For Bea," they said.

If she hadn't loved this town before, she did now.

Throughout the day, she looked for Bowie, missing him. Remembering the kiss. Praying to do the right thing, but yearning to see him just the same.

He never came.

Remembering the Bible verse, she resisted the longing to text or call.

*Love seeketh not its own.*

# *Chapter Twelve*

The rest of the week, Bowie was too busy to focus on anything but work. Late nights and long days made him haggard and edgy.

He feared he was losing ground.

A register cow and calf, attacked by predators, required frequent monitoring and treatment in barn 3. Three more calves were missing, their mamas bellowing and losing weight as they ran all over the pasture searching for their babies.

"Rustlers," Wade had said grimly. "Small-timers."

He'd called the county sheriff, though both Trudeau men strongly suspected the Keno boys were at it again. At least once a year, the Sundown lost a few head. They'd come to expect it, to write it off as the price they paid for their land bordering that of their archenemies.

Later, some of the cattle were found on Keno land, a result, the Kenos declared, of the Trudeau's lousy fencing efforts, not theft.

All of this meant he, Wade and Riley had miles and miles of fence line to drive or ride in case a Keno had gotten his laughs by cutting fence or opening gates. The job wasn't hard but it took time.

And stressed him.

Then there were his usual friendship chores. Cleaning gutters for an elderly friend who had no business climbing a ladder. Repairing Miss Beasley's outdated furnace for the fourth time before the cold weather set in. Paying a visit to

Jinx and his new puppies to install the promised cameras, hoping to catch a good shot of the mysterious stranger.

As much as he'd wanted to see Sage, he figured the Lord had sent him an especially busy week on purpose to get his mind off Sage and the fool he'd made of himself by kissing her.

Sometime around two o'clock in the morning, he laid aside his tools and carefully covered the latest leather design. He had to get some sleep. Ryder was coming out on Saturday. A cranky, exhausted man would not be beneficial to a troubled boy.

When Saturday arrived, Bowie felt almost human. This time, he'd left the workshop shortly after midnight and grabbed six full hours of sleep in his regular bed.

Every muscle in his shoulders and neck screamed from long hours at the workbench.

As Jinx liked to say, he'd bitten off more than he could chew and now he was choking on it.

After driving to Ms. Bea's home, he dropped off a spaghetti chicken casserole prepared by Wade's new wife and waited for Ryder to come down the stairs. Sage, he knew, was at the bakery, both a relief and disappointment.

He missed her.

But if she'd wanted him around, she'd have called or texted after that disastrous, wonderful kiss. Instead, she'd gone silent.

He got the message. Leave her alone.

In the living room of the rambling two-story, Ms. Bea sat in her recliner, looking as if she'd gone eight rounds with Mike Tyson.

Bowie took the couch opposite her. "How are you, Ms. Bea?"

"Ready to get out of this house." When his eyebrows went up, she circled a hand in front of her bruised face. "Never mind the way I look. It doesn't hurt. Who's minding my store with Sage today?"

"Becky and Shawna." His two good friends, who'd come to know Sage in Bible study, had eagerly volunteered their Saturday morning at the bakery. "They said it would be fun."

"God bless them. Such sweet girls." She motioned to a cane leaning against a side table. "Don't tell Sage or Doc West, but we won't need volunteers much longer. I'm hobbling around the house with that thing. Monday I'm going to work. I doubt I can do much except get in the way, but I can visit and give orders."

"Are you sure you're ready?"

"Don't fuss at me, Bowie. I'm getting old. I know it. My body's trying to quit on me, but I like to think I'm still needed."

"This town will always need you, Ms. Bea, and not only as their favorite baker. If you insist on getting back to work, how about a wheelchair?" When she started to protest, he raised a hand. "Temporarily."

"I guess that would be okay. Being old and useless is the worst feeling in the world."

"You're not useless, but it wouldn't hurt you to slow down some."

"I know it. Doc says the arthritis is progressing rapidly. Even with meds and staying active, I'm losing ground. Not complaining, now. Understand that. The Lord has been good to me and whatever comes my way, He'll help me handle it."

"I believe that."

"Which is why I'm thankful He sent Sage right when I needed her most. Bless her heart. She's a true godsend."

"Has she said anything about staying?" He looked down at the hat in his hands. "Permanently?"

"No. But I'm praying about pressing the matter. Something's on her mind. Something that makes her restless, anxious. Maybe she's told you and I don't know it, but she's like a hummingbird who can't land for very long."

As much as it bothered him, he'd thought the same thing. "Sage was always restless, afraid to settle."

"You know why."

He did. At least, in part.

"I think it's more than her unstable childhood this time, Bowie."

"Any ideas?"

"I hoped you'd know. She's closer to you than anyone."

He didn't know what to say to that.

Bea took a sip of something in a Sonic cup. Apparently, he wasn't her first visitor this morning. "Before you fetch Ryder and take off to your ranch, let's talk a minute."

"I thought we were."

She tilted her cup at him. "About you and Sage. Are you in love with her?"

That was Ms. Bea. Cut to the chase. "We're good friends."

"I see things differently. Sage is scared of something, holding back, for reasons she doesn't explain. And yet, who does she call, who does she run to, when something goes wrong? Or when something goes right, for that matter."

"Like I said, friends."

Bea tilted her head back and groaned. "Until you speak up, that's all you'll ever be. Sometimes you have to put yourself out there, Bowie."

"I don't want to lose her friendship."

Another groan. "If I'd had a son, I'd want him to be exactly like you. Except for one thing."

"What's that?"

She paused as if carefully considering her words.

"This old baker knows a bit of psychology, Bowie Trudeau. You and Sage have the same trauma, though you each handle it your own way. You're afraid of being abandoned again. The way your mama did you. The way Sage did when you were both too young and immature to know better. Even Heather and Brent and young Trent abandoned you, though not of their choosing. Now, Yates is gone to who-knows-where. All that loss takes a toll."

Her spot-on observation made him uncomfortable. He stared at the fencing scrapes on the backs of his hands and said nothing. He didn't like her thinking of him as some pitiful, broken orphan boy.

"All right, all right." Bea clumped her paper cup onto the end table. "I've said too much. You think about it—let the Lord talk to your spirit. Sage is worth it. So are you. You're better together, whether you know it yet or not."

While he pondered Ms. Bea's insights, he heard footsteps on the stairs and looked up as Ryder and Paisley entered the living room.

The two munchkins were a reprieve from a troubling, yet revealing, discussion he did not want to have.

"Morning, Ryder." Bowie rose. "Ready to go? We'll stop in town and take breakfast with us."

The boy worried the strings on his blue hoodie. "Can Paisley come?"

Ms. Bea spoke up. "Ryder, we talked about this. Paisley and I are going to play nurse and patient. She's going to be my helper today. Right, Paisley?"

Wearing a pleased expression, Paisley nodded and came to stand beside the older woman. Ms. Bea looped her arthritic hand with the little girl's.

Ryder gazed from the girls to Bowie. Then, recognizing the united front, he gave a sigh of resignation and headed toward the door.

Neither of them said much. Silence suited Bowie. Apparently, it suited Ryder too.

Once inside the sprawling, neat-as-a-pin workshop Bowie showed the boy some simple beginner projects he'd set up for today. A keychain, a cell phone cover, a bracelet. "Take your pick."

Ryder pointed at the bracelet. "Can I make one for Aunt Sage?"

"Great idea."

Ryder's face went from interested to troubled. "I should probably make one for my mom first, but I don't know where she is."

"Tell you what." Bowie laid out a thin strip of leather, already dyed and cut to appropriate size. He always had scraps for little projects like this. "Make one today. We'll make the other next time."

Ryder blinked up at him. A sandy brown rooster's tail stuck up on the back of his head. "I get to come back?"

"If you want to."

"Yeah. Maybe."

Following Bowie's lead, Ryder folded the strip in half and applied leather glue. The process was messy and the boy giggled sweetly when his fingers stuck together.

There was something so endearing about the boy, something that spoke to a deep place in Bowie. He prayed he could be the mentor Ryder needed.

Which meant Sage had to stick around town. An argument he'd use if the topic of leaving arose.

Bowie was wiping the boy's fingers with solvent when Ryder defaulted to worry about his sister. "Can Paisley come next time?"

He paused, holding Ryder's index finger inside the cloth. "Ms. Bea and Sage take good care of her, Ryder."

"Yeah. Maybe. She said she wanted to stay there today. I guess she's not afraid."

"Sage and Ms. Bea are kind to you, aren't they? They don't hurt you or Paisley, do they?"

"No. They're real nice. Sage snuggles with me and Paisley when Paisley gets scared. Sometimes she sleeps on the floor with me."

Envisioning a play tent made of sheets, Bowie chuckled. "Why were you on the floor? Camping out?"

Ryder's face remained serious. "Sometimes I sleep by Paisley's bed so she won't be scared."

Bowie thought his heart might come out of his chest. "And Sage sleeps with you? On the floor?"

"Yeah. That's real nice of her. Mama never did that, even when Paisley cried and cried."

His gut knotted.

"Why was Paisley crying? What scared her?" Bowie held his breath, pretending disinterest as he set out the leather punch and stamps for Ryder to choose. "Did something bad happen?"

Ryder nodded. Bowie waited. The boy needed to talk, to purge whatever fears he'd built so tall in his mind that he couldn't relax.

"Arlie was mean. He didn't like us."

Still quiet, still building a comfort zone to let Ryder feel free to talk, Bowie handed the boy a daisy tooling stamp.

Ryder studied the example bracelet, watching as Bowie showed him how and where to stamp the simple design.

Bowie took up his own project and worked beside the boy. With Bowie's gentle persuasion and in an atmosphere of acceptance, Ryder began to talk.

The story that unfolded filled Bowie with rage. He thought he might vomit. Or get in his truck and go hunting for a thug named Arlie.

"We have to talk."

Sage looked at the intense cowboy. She'd known from the moment he'd brought Ryder home that evening that something was wrong.

Ryder seemed fine. In fact, better than fine. He'd made her a sweet bracelet stamped with a daisy design that he'd proudly presented to her. She'd put it on and wore it now.

She'd been touched by the gift but thrilled by the relaxed expression her nephew wore. He'd sailed into the house, shot a glance at Paisley, but instead of hovering over her, he'd presented Sage with the bracelet and breathlessly filled her in on all the wonderful things he'd done that day with Bowie.

Bowie had come inside with him, ducking as he walked under Ms. Bea's ceiling fan, lingering as if he had something to say.

Sage ordered a pizza for dinner and he'd stayed, eating little, saying less. He was always quiet, but tonight he was tense, troubled.

Now that the kids had gone off to play and Ms. Bea watched TV in the living room, he wanted to talk.

What in the world had happened?

He jerked a thumb toward the porch. She followed him out and they settled in the swing.

Bowie, his feet planted firmly on the wooden porch, leaned forward, forearms on his thighs, hands clasped before him.

"What's wrong, Bowie? Did Ryder do something he shouldn't have?"

Instead of answering the direct question, he had one of his own.

He turned his head toward her. "How much do you know of his life with Amy?"

She tensed. Had he learned some terrible thing she should have known about?

"I've told you what I know. We were in different states. She'd answer my texts sometimes and send me snapshots of the kids if I asked. She never told me what was going on in her life. I rarely even knew where they were living."

"Or with whom." His tone was grim.

Sage's heart made one strong, hard beat that hurt her chest. "He told you something."

"Yeah."

"Bad?"

"Yeah." Bowie sucked in a long breath and sat back in the swing. The old wood groaned with his weight. "Some guy named Arlie. Amy's boyfriend, I assume."

Her mouth went dry. She'd heard too many horror stories about druggie boyfriends. "He's her latest boyfriend and meth supplier. A real creep."

"According to Ryder, Arlie didn't like him or Paisley. There wasn't much food in the house. Ryder would sneak what he could, but they went hungry, Sage."

Sage squeezed her eyes shut, fighting down a sudden sickness. "I was afraid of that."

"That's not the worst of it. Paisley cried a lot. She's little. A hungry kid cries. A scared kid cries. A kid without heat in the winter cries. Her crying infuriated Arlie."

She wasn't sure she could bear to hear the rest. Yet, she had to know.

"What happened?"

"This Arlie character was mean to them. He told them to be invisible. He didn't want to see them or hear them. One peep and they were in trouble. When Paisley cried he locked her in a dark closet. Sometimes all night or all day. Ryder tried to let her out a few times, but Arlie caught him and twisted his arms until he screamed."

Sage covered her face with her hands. "Oh, Bowie. No, no."

"Is it any wonder that she refuses to make a sound now to anyone except Ryder? She's afraid if she makes any noise, she'll end up in a dark closet, alone, hungry, scared."

"Where was Amy when this was happening to her children?"

"Asleep." Bowie put air quotes around the word, the expression on his face dark as night. Angry.

Another stab to the gut. "Passed out."

"Likely. Ryder's loyal to her, as you'd expect. None of it, in his eyes, was her fault. When Amy woke up she'd let Paisley out of the closet and fight with Arlie. She couldn't stop him, though. He was the boss."

"My own sister. To let that happen to her babies. She should have left him. Why didn't she leave?"

A muscle in Bowie's hard-as-concrete jaw flexed. "Drugs. Arlie was her supplier. The drugs were more important than the safety of her kids."

He spat the words as though they were rattlesnake venom. In a way, they were. Drugs poisoned all who fell under their spell, including the innocent victims like Ryder and Paisley.

"I feel sick and angry and helpless." She fought tears. She, who rarely cried, would cry for these precious children. "I'm so mad."

"Me too."

She gripped the porch swing chain with all the fury rising in her, threatening to boil over and do something drastic. "I will never allow Ryder and Paisley to be put in that situation again. No matter what I have to do."

"They're safe here. This is the best place for them to heal. With people like us who love them and with friends who care."

"I hope we can stay. I want to." With each passing day, she wanted that more and more. She loved working with Bea in the bakery. She enjoyed her new and old friends, especially Bowie. Losing him again would take a chunk out of her soul. A big chunk.

*Love seeks not its own.*

"You can." He shifted toward her. "Just do it. Stay. Settle. I'll help you every way I can."

His heart was in his voice. This good man cared for her as more than a friend, and she no more deserved him than Ryder and Paisley deserved to be mistreated.

Ms. Bea's words floated around in her head. Bowie loved her.

Aching, troubled, she suspected she loved him too. The emotion had been creeping up on her since the moment they'd reconnected.

With Bowie she was secure, happy. What would it be like to settle down with this big cowboy and make a real life for herself and Amy's kids in this small town that had welcomed them with open arms? The way Bowie had.

Utopia.

Her hopes plummeted.

Utopia didn't exist.

Even though she ran from the past, it was still out there, waiting to catch her.

She licked her dry lips. "Life isn't always that simple."

Bowie's arm dropped from the back of the swing to her shoulders and gave a gentle tug. "Maybe it is."

She leaned her head against him and murmured, "You always know what to do."

He did. She didn't.

"I'm here for you, Sage. I'm not going anywhere. Whatever you need."

What she needed was reassurance that life here could be everything it seemed to promise. That the kids would not be taken from her. That she could leave her mistakes, her baggage behind. That she could remain in Sundown Valley and make a life here. A permanent one.

She needed this town, this man.

But if Bowie knew everything, he wouldn't be so generous.

Now that she understood what the children had been through, at least in part, she would run to the far corners of the world to keep them away from their mother.

Because love did what was best for others.

# *Chapter Thirteen*

Rain washed the wide, undulating landscape overlooking the valley, painting an impressionist's watercolor of Oklahoma's late autumn. The wipers on Bowie's truck kept a slow, steady rhythm to match his heart.

Being a rancher, Bowie didn't mind the rain. He'd learned to love it, especially soft rain like today's mist. Rain gave life to the land, to the animals. Rain refreshed and renewed, washing away the dirt and grime the way prayer did for the soul.

He'd done a lot of praying lately. About the contract and Isaiah House. For Ryder and Paisley. For Sage and Ms. Bea. The two women needed each other though one of them was too stubborn or broken to admit it.

On the other hand, he thought the children were doing a little better. Paisley still spoke only to Ryder, but she didn't cling to him constantly. Ryder had been to the ranch with Bowie twice more without her. He was quite the little student in the leather workshop. The art seemed to soothe him. Bowie understood that kind of release better than anyone.

Pulling the truck to a halt next to a cleared acre where he'd someday build a house, Bowie turned to his passenger. "Sorry about the rain."

She'd asked to see the property, and he'd chosen Sunday afternoon when neither of them worked. Honoring the Sabbath was a pact he'd made with the Lord long ago. Work only in an emergency.

The contract was nearing emergency status, but he'd jumped at the excuse to spend an afternoon with Sage.

Foolish man.

Pale green eyes moved from the windshield to him. "I like it too."

"I thought I remembered that." He reached in the back for a pair of umbrellas. "I brought slickers too."

She shook her head, as he'd expected of her, rejecting the slickers. "Remember when we use to run in the rain and chase the rainbows?"

He smiled, mood tender. Having made the choice to spend time with Sage whenever he could, he refused to fret too much over the contract. He'd get there. He had to.

Last night, he'd even invited her entire crew to a steak-house for dinner. Ms. Bea had cut him off at the pass, insisting she and the kids had other plans.

A born matchmaker was Bea Cunningham.

She was back at work, but turning more and more of the bakery over to Sage. She simply wasn't able anymore, sad for sure. He wondered if Sage realized how much of the load she now carried at the business. Ms. Bea supervised and worked the counter from a rolling chair. Sage did everything else.

Sage, the beautiful baker. He liked the sound of that. He liked stopping in to see her, using the old equipment and fresh doughnuts as a flimsy excuse.

No matter how much he told himself to back off, he didn't listen. That Sage agreed to his invitations was enough.

So last night and again this afternoon, he and Sage were alone together.

Their dinner had been fun and relaxing, a Texas kind of place with peanuts on the floor and TVs on the walls. If he'd known they'd be alone, he would have chosen someplace nicer, more romantic.

As it was, he'd kissed her goodnight. Not the startling kiss of before, but a sweet, tender, controlled sharing of affection. She'd patted his cheek and smiled into his eyes.

How he loved her.

Sage took an umbrella from him and reached for her door handle. With a twinkle in those surreal irises, she pumped her eyebrows. "Man up, Trudeau. Let's do this."

Grinning like an infatuated teenager, he met her in front of the truck, wishing she'd given him a chance to use his manners and open her door.

She twirled the umbrella and bumped his side with hers. "This is the spot for your house?"

A soft mist swirled around them and over the building site. "Someday. Hopefully." When the right woman loved him. "What do you think?"

"I think Wade is right. You've picked the best location on the ranch. I love that you didn't take out all the trees."

He knew how she felt about trees. Growing took too long to go cutting them down.

"You're like the trees, Bowie," she'd told him once long ago. "Solid as an oak, planted, steady."

He'd taken it as a compliment. But sometimes he wondered if she'd meant boring.

Holding their umbrellas close, shoulders touching, they walked around the building site and gazed out over the valley.

She pointed to the hazy, mist-shrouded mountains in the distance. Time had eroded the ancient Kiamichi, rounding the tops so that they were peaceful and inviting, a paradise for campers and hikers. "This view is amazing."

"Yeah." He'd thought she'd like it.

From the day he'd started thinking about building a house, he'd considered her likes and dislikes. Maybe it wasn't the smartest thing to do, but he liked knowing he would someday live in a house that pleased Sage. Even if she didn't live in it with him.

"Is there anything you'd change?"

"Nothing. The house plans fit the landscape, fit you."

"What about you? Do they fit you?"

He asked lightly, though he held his breath tight and full inside his chest while his pulse thudded against his collarbone.

She shifted toward him, tilting her chin the tiniest amount to meet him eye to eye. "If I were ever to build a house, it would be exactly like those plans and in a place exactly like this. It's the most perfect place I can imagine."

The sincerity in her words, in her expression emboldened him. Ms. Bea's urgings to speak up hammered in his head.

He struggled to find the words.

"You could, you know. You could have a place like this. Here in Sundown Valley."

Those weren't the words he wanted to say at all, but they were safer ground than the confession raging inside him, pounding for release.

Sage was afraid she knew what Bowie was trying to say. The problem was, she couldn't let him. She wanted to. Oh, how she wanted to. Just as she'd wanted to move into his arms last night and kiss him with the emotion that simply would not go away.

This property, the future dream home he planned by asking her opinion on every single detail, held far deeper meaning than he let on. She wasn't naïve. With Ms. Bea hounding away in her not-so-subtle ways and Bowie going out of his way to show her and the kids every kindness, she knew Bowie cared for her as more than a friend.

She felt the same.

And it scared her out of her mind.

All the what-ifs flew into her brain like buzzards come home to roost.

What if she admitted her feelings? What if she told Bowie she loved him, too? Then, suddenly, the authorities came for the children and she had to take them away, leaving him broken and bewildered? What if she went to jail? What if Bowie learned *everything* about her past?

How could she put him through that kind of humiliation?

Yet, what if they could make it work? What if she could go on forever hiding the children and her ugly past right here on the Sundown Ranch with Bowie?

*Love didn't seek its own way.*

But what about Bowie's needs and wants? Shouldn't she seek those?

She reached for his hand and started walking again, battling her tangled thoughts. His strong, calloused rancher's hand curled around her slender rain-cooled fingers, secure, comfortable. *Right.*

They walked on and he pointed out the place where he hoped to build a barn for his favorite horses. Two of the animals, their backs dark with moisture, grew curious about the humans and ambled over for a nose rub.

Bowie had a quiet way with them. They trusted him implicitly. So did she. Wasn't that enough?

Horses trailing along, they crossed the soft, wet grass to his workshop, located fifty yards or so from the future building site. He took her inside and showed her the crafts he and Ryder were creating.

She ran a fingertip over a butter-soft flat of golden leather. "Whatever you're saying to Ryder when you're together is helping."

"Mostly, I let him talk." He grinned. "With a little nudge now and then. He's figured out that he and Paisley are in good hands with you."

Her stomach clenched. She had to keep them that way. "With you too."

He tilted his head in acknowledgment. No false modesty from Bowie. He handled the boy with the same patience and tenderness he used on the horses that followed him like puppies.

She roamed the long building, taking in the tiny section where it was obvious he sometimes slept, although she focused on the tools and machinery, the pieces of dyed leather, the beautiful work in progress.

Most of it was covered, but some was visible.

A row of slots below his workbench held templates and drawings. She removed a handful and began to sort through them, admiring the intricate designs.

"You work from these?"

"Some. Some things I create on the fly."

Laying aside the image of a colorful dragonfly, her fingers froze.

"What's this?"

"What's what?" Bowie turned from sliding a pretty fringed handbag into a box. When he saw the painting in her hands, his mouth dropped. "Oh."

He reached for the painting. She yanked it back to gaze down at a much younger version of herself. "When did you do this?"

"Years ago. It's not very good."

He was wrong about that.

He'd captured her in a pose as free and wild as a running mustang. Racing toward some unseen finished line, her head was back, her long hair blowing behind her, her face turned to stare at the painter, green eyes gazing out with desperate hope.

"Did I really look this way to you?"

"You still do. Beautiful. Always running." He took the painting from her and slid it back into the slot.

She was both flattered and bothered. Flattered that he'd wanted to capture her in art. Bothered by the expression on her face that matched the turmoil inside her spirit.

As if uncomfortable that she'd seen the painting, he drew her attention to a project Ryder was working on. Sage let the subject of the painting drop, though it lingered in her thoughts.

After admiring Ryder's work, she turned to a long table where several pieces of something were covered.

"What are these?"

He hesitated, got a funny look on his face. "Projects I'm working on."

She stood in front of the table, tempted to lift each cover and have a peek. "You've done considerably more since the last time I was here."

"Yeah." He came up beside her, quiet as always, but with a tension she didn't understand. He rubbed a hand over the back of his neck, as if the tension came from there. "A lot."

"Are they Christmas gifts? I get the feeling you don't want to talk about them."

"I'd like to show them to you, but—"

Sage tilted her head, puzzled. "But what? What's going on, Bowie?"

With careful fingers, he uncovered the first project.

Sage gasped. "Bowie, that's exquisite work. Wow."

His shoulders relaxed. "Good. It has to be. Only the best will do for PJ Enterprises. They've contracted me to do ten of these, all original and handcrafted. No two alike."

She turned a stunned look from the leatherwork to his face. In her short, painful stint in the modeling industry, she'd learned plenty about high-end companies, including this one. "PJ Enterprises? I've heard of them. They deal in super expensive products for major top-shelf retailers."

"That's what I hear."

"So, what's going on? Tell me. This sounds exciting."

He told her of the phone call, the contract and the money he could earn if all went well.

"Not that I need money for myself, but I'll donate these first earnings to Isaiah House. If they contract me for more next year, I can do more. Maybe even start building my house."

He'd told her of his love for the New Orleans shelter where he'd lived briefly as a boy.

A contract of this caliber could prove enormous.

"This is amazing, fabulous!" She grabbed his arms and happy danced him around the concrete floor.

Laughing, he stopped her in midpolka. "Don't get too excited. I have to finish the projects before December 16. I've a ways to go."

"December 16? That's less than three weeks away."

He huffed a short grunt. "Don't remind me. If I don't make the deadline, I lose the contract and Isaiah House may close. I can't let that happen."

"Then you have to finish these purses and whatever else you're doing for PJ. The kids and I will help any way we can. Tell us what you need."

"It's art, Sage. I'm the only one who can create them and truly call them mine."

That he was in this situation alone bothered her, but she didn't know what to do to help. She could add fancy icing to a cupcake. She knew nothing about crafting a leather purse.

By the time they were outside again, the rain had cleared and the sun pushed aside the clouds. Sunshine after the rain.

Her head still whirled with excitement over Bowie's contract. She wanted this for him. Wanted it so bad. And she knew with confidence that he had the talent to succeed.

"I'm so proud of you." She grabbed his hand, grinned at him and started toward the truck. He grinned in return.

Their boots squishing against the sodden ground, Bowie stopped and pointed. "A rainbow. God's promise."

She loved rainbows. Bowie knew that.

"Let's chase it," he said. "Like we used to."

"Shouldn't you take me home so you can work on your projects?"

"Nope. Not on Sunday."

She'd almost forgotten his devotion to the Lord's day of rest.

"Okay, then, mister." Sage jabbed a finger toward the colorful arch. "Let's find that pot of gold."

Bowie laughed. "Race you to the truck."

Sloshing and splashing over the wet terrain, they arrived at the truck simultaneously and collapsed against the hood. Breath puffing, they grinned at each other.

"You cheated," she said.

He laughed and opened her door. She hopped in and he rounded the truck, slapping a jaunty palm against the hood before climbing into the driver's seat.

"Pot of gold here we come."

Laughing and making silly jokes about what they'd do with all that gold, Bowie aimed his truck up curving, gravel roads, around hills and low mountains, following the bright colors arched against the skyline.

They drove for miles. Still, they could not reach the rainbow's end.

Finally, Bowie pulled into an overlook and killed the engine.

Leaning an arm on the steering wheel, he turned toward her. "We're never going to find it."

"Phooey. I was so looking forward to that pot of gold and a castle in the Alps."

Bowie's soft gaze turned serious. "Would that make you

happy, Sage? Would that make you want to settle down and stay in one place?"

"You know I was only joking." She touched the knee he'd propped on the seat. "Haven't you ever wanted to live anywhere else?"

"I've lived somewhere else."

Of course he had. His childhood had been worse than hers. "I didn't mean—"

"I know what you meant." He motioned toward the hills and valleys sprawling around them. "When Brett and Heather brought me here, a scraggly kid who barely knew right from wrong, this place became a refuge I didn't know I was looking for. Oh, I could go chasing after rainbows, searching for what I don't have, but I'm grateful God saw fit to plant me right here in this beautiful place. There is no pot of gold, Sage. Treasure is where your heart is."

"Yours is here."

"The Bible says to be content where I am with what I have. Did you know the apostle Paul was on death row in a Roman prison when he wrote that?"

"I didn't."

"Even in a dark dungeon, about to face death, he was content. Joyful even." He patted the top of her hand. "Chasing rainbows is fun. But it won't give us that."

"You are a wise soul, Bowie Trudeau." She sighed, wishing she could settle down right here in these ancient mountains and build a life. With him.

What he didn't understand, what she could not explain, was that for once in her life she wanted to grow roots. Her restless heart wasn't the problem anymore.

Opening the truck door, she stepped out and walked to the railing that kept cars and people from plummeting over the edge to the rocky, brushy terrain below. Bowie's boots crunched as he came up beside her.

She gripped the metal rail. It was damp from the rain.

Gazing at the rainbow arched somewhere in the distance, out of reach, she pondered Bowie's words.

Rainbows, a hopeful sign from God. A promise.

"Bowie." She kept her eyes glued to the rainbow, clinging to hope.

"Yes." His shoulder touched hers as he swiveled in her direction. She could feel his sincere gaze on her.

"I—care for you. A lot."

The air around them stilled. Bowie was quiet for a dozen thudding heartbeats.

When he spoke, the sound was a gentle murmur. Gentle and quiet like the man. "I care for you too. Always have."

"I thought so. The painting. The house plans. Everything you've done for the kids and me. It's more than a friendship, isn't it?"

"That's up to you."

*Learn to be content with what you have where you are.*

She had so much to appreciate in Sundown Valley.

*Love seeks not its own.*

Her problem wasn't contentment. Not anymore.

His arm went around her from the side. She leaned into him. Stalwart Bowie. A refuge.

Slowly, she turned to face him, gazing at the man who had always been there for her. She bracketed his face with both hands, leaned in and kissed him.

He laughed softly. And then he kissed her back.

She didn't let herself think about all the worrisome what-ifs.

# *Chapter Fourteen*

Wade sipped at his coffee cup and stared at Bowie. "What's wrong with you this morning? I just told you that cattle prices have crashed. We stand to lose a significant chunk of money. But you sit there munching your bacon, not the least perturbed."

Kyra, toddlers in footed pajamas following her around the dining room like three little ducks, paused next to her husband's chair and kissed him on the ear. "Bowie never looks perturbed."

Bowie hitched a shoulder. "Nothing I can do about livestock prices."

"You could complain a little with me."

Wade's comment tickled him. His cousin, a crackerjack businessman, sometimes let the unpredictable ebb and flow of the livestock market drive him up the wall. Prices rose. They fell. The Sundown Ranch would survive and thrive.

"I'm commiserating," he said. Nobody liked losing money, especially a man in need of a lot of it. Wade had just given him another reason to push hard on his leather contract.

"See, honey. He's commiserating." Kyra settled a baby in a booster seat.

Wade hopped out of his chair to help with the other two. First, he grabbed his new wife and danced her around the kitchen. "You make everything better."

She did.

They made a good team, these two—helpmates, partners, the way the Bible said a man and woman should be.

Since Kyra had come into his life, Wade was a different man. Content, fulfilled.

Bowie polished off another bacon strip. He was also content. Fulfillment was a different matter.

However, things were looking up. Sage cared for him. She hadn't used the word love, but neither had he. Not yet.

But he believed they were moving toward something beautiful, something permanent.

He loved her enough for both of them. Having her return that love would be a dream come true. Like Wade and Kyra. He wanted that kind of forever.

After those pretty amazing kisses the other night, he'd planned to take her somewhere really nice for dinner this weekend, but, with the PJ deadline nearing, he'd resisted asking. He was, however, glad he'd told her about the contract. Her enthusiastic response had given him a boost of confidence he hadn't known he needed.

He'd agreed to spaghetti and meatballs at Bea's house tonight, but he would leave early and hit the workshop until the wee hours. In fact, leaving early had been her idea. He knew she was trying to be thoughtful of his time, but it bothered him that she'd been the one to make the suggestion.

The little fear that lived in the back of his brain crept into his consciousness. They weren't a couple. Not yet anyway. She'd made no declarations or promises.

Did she still have leaving on her mind?

She cared about him. *Cared*, but he felt her love in the things she did for him, the thrill she expressed in his future with PJ Enterprises.

He clung to the last thoughts. She cared. For him, this town, Ms. Bea.

She was happy in the bakery. She'd even begun baking specialty breads, one for each day of the week. They sold, she told him with a glow of pride, like hotcakes at a church breakfast.

He was proud of her.

Sage was more than beautiful. She was smart, thoughtful, hardworking.

Pushing him away tonight was her method of giving him time in his workshop, not a brush-off.

"He's got that look," he heard Kyra say.

Bowie tuned back in to the conversation. They'd caught him daydreaming about Sage.

"Uh-huh." Wade pointed a drippy coffee spoon at him. "What gives with you and Sage? Have you finally told her how you feel?"

Abby, seated next to Bowie in a booster chair, offered him a slice of banana. He popped it in his mouth. Baby hands didn't bother him anymore.

He wondered how many kids Sage wanted? He didn't know the full story on Ryder and Paisley but if they were a package deal, he'd consider them a gift. He knew the importance of love and family for kids coming out of trauma.

Kyra rose from the table and refilled her coffee cup. Hoisting the carafe in Bowie's direction, she raised an eyebrow in question.

Bowie shook his head. "No more for me."

He was so jazzed up on caffeine in order to keep working late every night, his head buzzed.

"You could answer my question, you know." Wade popped a piece of bacon into his mouth with one hand and wiped a baby's face with the other.

The action tickled Bowie. His cousin had become adept at multitasking with toddlers.

"We're seeing each other. I'm pretty busy. So's she."

The carafe clinked back onto the heat source. Kyra

walked past his chair and patted his shoulder. "Good for you. She's an awesome girl."

"Yeah." He pushed back his chair and rose.

"Heading to the bakery?" Wade drummed four fingers over the left side of his blue shirt, like a beating heart.

Bowie let a pleased grin slide up his face. "The vet clinic."

Wade read his mind and laughed. "Bring back some pecan rolls. The sticky caramel kind."

For Sage, the days sailed past.

Thanksgiving had come and gone. Then, according to Ms. Bea, the crazy season began in full force.

Sage was hard-pressed to imagine how much busier things could get.

She tore a piece from a freshly baked loaf of lemon cranberry bread. "Try this, Ms. Bea, and see if I got it right."

Bea took the sample and looked it over. "Crumb is excellent." She popped it in her mouth and chewed thoughtfully. Her brown eyes widened. "Perfection. Give me another bite."

Sage laughed, pleased.

"You're becoming quite the bread baker." Bea rolled her chair to the refrigerator and took out a bowl of butter.

The pride Sage felt in baking bread surprised her. She loved working and shaping the dough, tasting the results, experimenting with different recipes and spices.

For someone who'd once dreamed of fame and fortune as a supermodel, reveling in fancy breads seemed completely out of character.

After becoming a follower of Jesus, her perspective on life had changed. She was growing in her faith, thanks to Ms. Bea and regular church attendance. Her foster mom claimed God had a perfect plan for each of our lives, but it's up to us to seek Him until we know what that plan is.

Did His plan include this town and baking bread for her community? Was Bowie part of God's plan?

She was starting to believe, to hope, to pray, that he was.

Yet, a painful truth nagged in the back of her mind, needing release but holding back because of the kids. They were small, vulnerable innocents. They had to come first, even before her feelings for Bowie.

She longed to tell Bowie everything about her past and about the kids, but was confession the right thing, the loving thing to do? Was dumping that ugly knowledge in his lap fair to him?

If she was truthful, shame held her back as well. Now that she'd fallen in love with Bowie, she didn't want to hurt him. She also didn't want to watch his love turn to disgust.

"The houska bread I made last week was a hit," she said, more to stop the disturbing thoughts than for conversation. "Customers asked for it again. Mary Pam stopped me after church to tell me how much her family loved my recipe, especially her Czech grandpa."

"I've always considered bread a special gift from God," Bea said as she slathered butter onto a slice of the raisin bread. "The Bible is loaded with bread references, you know. Jesus even called his body the bread of life. And God *did* feed the children of Israel on manna when they were wandering in the wilderness all those years."

"Was manna a type of bread?"

"I think so. Honey flavored."

Sage cocked a hand on a hip. "Sure wish I had that recipe."

Bea laughed. "God kept that one secret, but there are plenty of others."

"I know. It's so fun looking through ethnic recipes. I'm thinking stollen or panettone at Christmas. There are so many wonderful Christmas breads it's hard to decide."

Bea paused, the bread slice halfway to her lips. "Sounds like someone is settling in for the long haul."

"Maybe I am." And in Sundown Valley of all places. "Oh, Ms. Bea, I can't ever repay you for taking us in. The kids are improving, healing. I haven't found Ryder sleeping on the floor next to Paisley's bed in a long time. He's not such a helicopter brother anymore."

"Bless his heart."

"And Paisley's become my snuggle bug."

"I noticed that. Every time you sit down, she's in your lap."

"I love her. I love reading to her and her big brother. It's wonderful to see them beginning to relax."

"I could say the same about you."

Sage cocked her head, puzzled. "Me?"

"Look at you, honey. Running this bakery, adding new items to the menu. You've gotten involved at North Cross and made friends. And of course, there's that handsome Bowie."

"This town, and you, have been good to us."

"So has Bowie."

"Yes, he has."

Bea pointed her half-eaten bread. "You've fallen in love with him, haven't you? Exactly the way I hoped."

No use pretending otherwise. Not with Bea.

"It scares me, Ms. Bea," she admitted.

"Why, honey? Bowie Trudeau is the least scary man I know. He'll do right by you. That boy has cared for you since he was fifteen years old."

Sage shook her head. Her ponytail wobbled. "That's not what I mean. Bowie's wonderful."

"Then what is it? Why can't you let go and let God bless you with a good life in this fine little town with that fine Christian man who'd do anything to make you happy?"

Sage turned back to the cooling rack and took down a tray of bread to package into plastic bags.

She was tempted to tell Ms. Bea the whole story.

"I keep thinking the other shoe is going to drop."

Bea rolled her chair to the pass-through door and waved at an incoming customer.

Over one shoulder she said, "Trust God, honey. He's brought you this far. He has a plan, a perfect one. He's not going to let you down now."

As Ms. Bea rolled away, already chatting to the customer, Sage inhaled the warm fragrant bread, straightened her shoulders, and mole-whacked the anxiety trying to rear its ugly head.

Ms. Bea was right. God wouldn't let her down.

She and the kids were safe here. Bowie loved her. She loved him.

Everything would work out just fine.

A chilly December dawn broke over the Sundown Ranch as Bowie loped to his truck and hopped inside.

He was running late.

Last night, he'd worked until after midnight again. This morning he'd overslept. Burning the midnight oil had served him well. He was almost there. The projects, except for two, were complete, and the special order leather for those two was already cut.

He was going to make the deadline with quality workmanship he was proud to put his name on.

Back in business, he'd call Isaiah House sometime today and let Ian know the plumbing money would soon be headed his way.

Pulling up to the workshop, he hopped out, eager to get started.

The front of the building was dark.

Bowie frowned up at the security light above the doorway.

The bulb must have burned out during the night. He'd have to get that replaced.

Humming a praise tune, he approached the door. Suddenly, he froze. A chill slithered down his spine. He couldn't see anything out of place, couldn't put his finger on the problem, but something was wrong.

He reached for the doorknob. It turned easily in his hand.

Without the key.

Pulse jerking, he eased the door open. "Anyone in here?"

Nothing. No sound other than his own hoarse breathing.

He flipped on the lights.

And his heart stopped.

Twenty minutes later, the county sheriff was there to assess the damage. Wade had arrived in less than five.

Just having his cousin in the building helped, though at the moment, he was devastated.

"Someone made a real mess," the sheriff said.

"Yeah." Bowie raked a hand over his head.

Every cabinet, every drawer, every tool had been dumped on the floor. Leatherwork was scattered everywhere.

"Any of this valuable?"

"Some of it." He retrieved the piece of leather he'd cut last night. The expensive special order material was ruined, a large, muddy footprint stamped across what would have been the flap of a handbag. It made him sick to his stomach. "Very valuable."

Wade shot him a questioning glance. He waved him off. "I'll explain later."

His cousin nodded. "You suspect the same people I do?"

He nodded, adding, "We also have to consider the hobo we've spotted lurking around. The one I told you about.

First seen near your wedding and now he's been spotted again by several others, including me and Sage. Could have been him."

"Have you checked the security camera?"

Bowie nodded grimly. "Someone knew enough to duct tape the lens."

"Great. Just great." Wade scowled at the mess, fuming. "Is anything missing?"

"Can't tell. Won't know until I sort through all of this and put things where they belong."

"I'll stay and help. Moving pasture can wait until tomorrow."

Grimly, Bowie perched his hands on his hips, his chest heaving in one heavy breath. "Sheriff wants to get fingerprints first."

The sheriff looked up from snapping photos of the debris. "Mind if I take that leather you got there? We might be able to use that footprint."

Belly lower than a snake, Bowie handed over the piece. The leather itself was costly, but at least he hadn't yet put in hours tooling the design.

He gazed at the stack of handbags he'd retrieved from the floor. Were they salvageable?

Or should he just give up, call Katherine Pembroke, return the advance money, and let his dream die here on the dirty, debris-scattered floor?

After the sheriff left, Bowie told Wade about the contract, asking him to keep the news under his hat, especially now. He wanted his cousin to understand why this break-in mattered so much.

Wade cupped a hand to Bowie's shoulder. "Whatever you need, brother. Don't worry about the ranch. Riley and I can hold the fort for the next couple of weeks while you catch up in here."

"I don't know if I'll be able to." He was down. No use denying it. Having his shop ransacked, his leatherwork destroyed, had hit him hard. "Time's not on my side."

"Maybe not." Wade looked him in the eye. "But we are."

The reassurance buoyed him. He couldn't give up. He had to try.

With his cousin's careful help, Bowie began the task of sorting through the mess.

Thirty minutes later, Sage stormed through the door. "What on earth happened? Who did this?"

She looked so fierce, Bowie offered a sad smile. "You gonna wring somebody's neck for me?"

She made a wrenching motion with her hands. "I'd like to. When Wade texted me, I couldn't believe it. All your hard work, all these beautiful bags and wallets." She clenched her teeth and shuddered. "Ooh, I'm so mad."

Wade chuckled. "Remind me not to get her riled."

She sure was beautiful when she was defending her people. An Amazonian warrior, just like in the movies.

"I'm pretty mad myself."

Squinting at him, she said, "You don't look mad. You look devastated."

Bowie tilted his head. "That works."

She walked right up to him and slid her arms around his waist and leaned against him. "I'm sorry, babe. So, so sorry. I know what this means to you."

Wade cleared his throat. "I think I should go check cows or something. Leave you two alone. Call me if you need me."

Bowie lifted a hand from Sage's shoulder and waved his cousin away. Wade couldn't help. He knew nothing about leather crafting. No one could help.

Except maybe Sage.

"Thank you for coming out here," he murmured against her hair. "You make me feel better."

"That's my line. You're the one who rescues everybody."

Except himself.

She pulled back to stare around the room, still fuming. Because of him. For his sake. Because she cared, and that caring felt a lot like love.

"What can you salvage?"

He and Wade had made some progress, but the place was still a mess.

"Quite a bit, I think. Wade and I found all of the PJ products." He pointed to a table he'd cleared. "Two are ruined and two are not yet finished. The others appear to be unharmed."

"So, you have four projects to complete between now and December 16."

He scrubbed a hand over his face. "Unless a problem shows up on one of the other six."

"Okay." She moved around the shop, taking long, graceful strides that distracted him from the carnage of his dream. "If you do nothing but focus on the contracted bags for the remaining time, can you make the deadline?"

"Maybe. But I have other obligations. I can't spend every waking moment out here."

"What if you can? What if the rest of the world leaves you alone? I mean, *everyone*. So you have nothing to do but this."

"Then I'd make that deadline or die trying."

She plopped out a long-fingered hand. "Give me your cell phone."

Bowie never knew for certain what Sage had done, but suddenly, his phone stopped ringing, his texts stopped pinging and the only people who ever entered his workshop were Wade or Sage. Wade even brought his clothes and meals to the shop so that he didn't have to go home unless he wanted to.

The only time he took a real break was the night of Sundown Valley's Christmas Parade. The church entered a float every year. This year, Ryder and Paisley were part of the children's choir riding on that float.

He wouldn't have missed their moment for anything.

Waiting on the sidewalk outside the bakery, he huddled deep in his fleece-lined jacket. Next to him Sage hopped up and down, trying to keep warm.

He was exhausted. His eyes burned. His body ached. After the days stuck inside, he welcomed the fresh air.

To signal the start of the parade, a police car drove slowly past, blaring a siren down Main Street.

Sage stopped bouncing and leaned closer, voice lifted. "How's the work going?"

"Never mind that. I've missed you."

"Me too. You've been working nonstop. No interruptions?"

Using any excuse to touch her, he tugged her hood up. "None. I wonder how that happened."

Sage only smiled and slid an arm around his waist to snuggle close. "Cold out here."

"Uh-huh." He covered her shoulders with his thickly jacketed arm. "Gotta stay warm."

She chuckled, pale eyes bright as the high school band marched past with a cheerful rendition of "God Rest Ye Merry Gentlemen."

"The floats are next." She pointed. Her height, like his, gave her an advantage over the other townsfolk gathered in front of the business.

Occasionally, someone popped into the bakery for a coffee or to get warm. He noticed the way Sage kept a close eye through the window to be sure Ms. Bea didn't need her.

The older woman had come to depend on Sage.

So had he. He realized how much when she'd somehow cleared his schedule, gotten friends from the church to cover his widow errands and even regimented how long the two of them spoke on the phone each night.

He'd laughed and called her a control freak, but in truth, he was grateful beyond words.

Her text messages, which ended with heart emojis and funny gifs, had kept him going.

He ended his with *Love, Bowie.*

"Deadline's on Tuesday," he said, paying more attention to her than the passing float of Santa's workshop complete with school-age elves.

Sage turned her eyes to his. "And?"

He let the smile come.

"I'm going to make it." He kissed her nose. "Because of you."

# *Chapter Fifteen*

Sage stood at the bakery counter discussing a donation to the Christmas Bazaar, a fundraiser put on by the police and fire departments to provide Christmas for local foster children.

Sundown Valley, she'd learned, pulled out all the stops for the holidays, everything from parades, and pageants to the city-wide bazaar.

Along Main Street, garlands and bright red bows turned the streetlights into cheerful glowing candy canes. Santa and nativity scenes appeared in shop windows.

The festive atmosphere put a bounce in everyone's steps and smiles on faces.

The season was glorious, filled with love and hope. So was Sage.

Today Bowie would ship the handbags to PJ Enterprises. He'd made his deadline. Tonight he was coming over to celebrate.

Whipping out her phone, she texted a quick, Can't wait to see you. Love, Sage.

She'd missed him terribly these last weeks, a loneliness that opened her eyes to true love. Love like Bowie displayed. Love God's way.

She was happy here. The kids were more secure than they'd probably ever been.

Sundown Valley had become home.

Home where people did wonderful things like buying Christmas gifts for foster families.

"This is a project near to my heart," Sage told the perky red-haired wife of police chief Adam. "My sister and I were foster kids with Ms. Bea."

"Adam mentioned that. He said you'd understand the importance of the bazaar."

"He's right. What do you suggest we donate?"

"The specialty breads. Anything Christmassy would sell especially well this time of year. Your breads are so good, Sage. Ms. Bea says you're the one making them now, not her."

"A labor of love." But she was thrilled at the compliments. Some even claimed her bread was better than Bea's but those were comments she kept tucked inside. "How many loaves can you sell?"

"We'll take all you have time for. Can I put you down for twenty?"

"Done."

She'd have to work late for several nights, but the idea of providing Christmas for needy children filled her with joy. She'd been on the other side. She'd done without a gift on more than one Christmas morning. No child would experience that disappointment if she could help it.

The thought brought her to her niece and nephew. Had they ever done without Christmas? The idea stabbed at her. She should have been there for them. She should know the answer, but she didn't.

The police chief's wife left. Customers came and went. Bea worked the front and Sage made small batches of fresh cookies and doughnuts throughout the day.

In the afternoon, the sun elbowed its way through the clouds, and passersby shed their jackets.

A chilly, sunny, perfect December day.

Humming to herself, Sage mentally counted her money, budgeting the amount she could spend on Christmas gifts.

Other than purchasing basic needs, she'd saved most of

her paychecks. Neither of the kids had asked for a thing, which caused an ache somewhere in her midsection. She aimed to see they had the best Christmas of their lives.

When the lively, Christmas-charged after-school crowd dwindled, Sage and Bea began the closing chores.

With milk and cookies at his elbow, Ryder sat at the bistro table in the back working on homework. Paisley sprawled on the floor on her belly, paging through a picture book about the first Christmas while she munched an oatmeal cookie. She loved hearing about Baby Jesus.

When Sage paused in putting away baking sheets to watch them, love filling her, Ryder glanced up and smiled.

That smile was worth a million dollars to her. She crossed the space and smoothed a hand over his persistent rooster tail. "I love you, Ryder."

Paisley looked up, catching Sage's attention.

"You, too, Princess Paisley." She took hold of one of Paisley's puppy dog ponytails and tickled it over the child's cheek.

The little girl's eyes danced with pleasure before she returned her attention to Baby Jesus.

*Please take away her fear. Show her it's okay to talk to other people.*

Leaving the duo and Ms. Bea in the kitchen, she went into the front to answer the bell.

Mark Feldman, ears red from the cold, shoulders hunched inside his suit jacket, brought the smell of December all the way to the register.

"Hi, Mr. Feldman. What can I do for you?" She motioned to the display case. "Not a lot left, but they're still fresh and the price is right."

"Four of those cream cheese cupcakes sound good."

"An inspired choice, I'm sure," she teased as she reached for a small to-go carton.

"Actually, Sage, I stopped by to talk to you about something."

Sage paused, one gloved hand on a cupcake. "About the kids?"

"Yes."

"Is Ryder in trouble?"

"No. Not at all. He's doing fine. He's really fond of his teacher, though, and she shared some troubling things that he told her."

Sage's pulse began to pound. "They're coming out of a lot of trauma."

"Yes, but it's not only that. You see, Ryder said that when his mother went to jail, a man came to the apartment to take him and Paisley to foster care."

"Right." Heat boiled up in her chest, rose on her neck. Panic came with it. She batted it down, kept her focus on slowly choosing the perfect cupcakes. "Thank goodness, I showed up in time to prevent that from happening. Kinship takes precedence."

That much she knew was true. She'd heard the term many times. Hadn't social services spent years trying to find suitable relatives to take her and Amy after their parents died? So many wasted years searching meant they'd never been adopted.

"I understand that. So you gained guardianship?"

"Yes." She'd gained it by grabbing the kids and driving away.

The principal breathed a long sigh. "Good. Good. Kids get things confused and, when Mrs. Farmer sent him in to talk with me, he said a few things that had me worried." His lips curved. "He also says you are the best aunt in the world, and he loves you."

She grabbed onto that statement. "I'd do anything for those children, Mr. Feldman."

She had and she would again.

The principal nodded, seemingly mollified.

She handed over the box of cupcakes and took his money.

As he opened the shop door, he turned back toward her. "Tomorrow when you bring the kids to school, bring a copy of their guardianship papers by my office. A formality. We need those for their records."

The door sucked closed as he left, taking with him all the hope and security she'd found in the last few months.

Adrenaline jacked into her bloodstream.

*Run. Hurry.*

That's all she could think of. Take Ryder and Paisley and get away before Mr. Feldman realized she had no legal right to the kids. Before he called the authorities. Before she went to jail and the children went to strangers.

Heat flooded her face. Blood pounded in her head.

"Ms. Bea." The words quavered. She swallowed, pushing back the anxiety she heard in her own voice.

Bea appeared in the pass-through. "Something wrong, hon?"

*Breathe. Don't panic.*

"No, no. I was only—" her gaze went to the children "—wondering if you would mind finishing up here? I'll take Ryder and Paisley on home."

"Don't mind at all." The older woman looked concerned for a moment. Then her countenance brightened. "Bowie must be coming over tonight."

Sage licked dry lips.

*Oh, dear. He was.*

They'd planned a celebration.

In her shock of being discovered, she'd forgotten.

*Hurry. Go.* The words pushed at her chest, speeding up an already racing heart.

Pack the kids. Get out of town before Bowie arrives.

She grabbed onto Bowie as the excuse. “Yes. Do you mind?”

Bea flapped a hand at her. “Go on. The only thing left to do here is man the register until six and box up leftovers. I’m not too old and feeble to do that.”

“Oh, Ms. Bea. I didn’t mean any such thing.” She paused beside the dear woman for a side hug. “I love you. You’ve been such a gift to the kids and me.”

She wanted to apologize, to plead with Ms. Bea not to despise her for what she’d done. For leaving without so much as a goodbye. To tell her exactly how much she’d come to love her and this bakery and this town.

For a nanosecond, she was tempted to confess everything. Just blurt it out and face the consequences.

She didn’t, of course. If Ms. Bea knew about her past she’d be heartbroken. She’d also try to stop her from leaving.

Besides, she wasn’t the only one who faced the consequences of her actions. There were Ryder and Paisley to consider. They’d come too far to be taken away by strangers.

They were the important ones. No matter that she loved Bowie. No matter that she’d started to dream of forever in this sweet little town with that wonderful cowboy.

He’d be so humiliated, so angry if he knew what she’d done.

Bea patted her shoulder, returning the hug. “I love you too. Now, go on. Get prettied up for your man.”

Her man. The man who loved her, probably always had. And she loved him.

Now, she had to break his heart.

And her own.

“Why are you putting our stuff in the trash?”

Ryder stood in the doorway of his room watching Sage with suspicion.

"I'm not throwing things away, Ryder." She dumped his dresser drawer into the giant plastic trash bag. "We're going on a little trip."

"To see Mama?" He didn't look excited about the prospect.

"I don't know. Maybe." She didn't want to lie to him. "Probably not."

"Why do we have to go?"

Sage paused in the mad rush of throwing things into the sack. "Please, Ryder, don't fuss. Something's happened, and we have to leave Sundown Valley."

"I don't want to. I like it here." Expression dark and belligerent, he backed out of the room to stand in the hallway and glare at her.

He liked it here. That was the first time he'd admitted liking anything except Bowie and ice cream.

Paisley, terrified of conflict, must have heard the conversation. She appeared at her brother's side and clung to his hand.

Sage closed her eyes and prayed a short *help* prayer.

After all the progress the children had made, was she throwing them right back into chaos?

Losing them to strangers would be even worse, wouldn't it?

Going to the children, she drew them into a hug.

"I love you. I'll take care of you, just like before. We'll be okay. I promise."

Neither seemed convinced, but it was the best she could do for now.

Bowie and Ms. Bea would arrive soon. If she had to face either one, she might fold.

Then what would happen to these kids?

Racing into Paisley's room, she continued the same wild effort to cram clothes and toys into backpacks and the giant trash bag.

The children didn't follow her this time. Later, when

they were on the road, she'd try to explain. Or maybe she'd make a game of it like before. An adventure.

Ryder hadn't believed her then. He wouldn't now.

She hurried to her bedroom and tossed everything she owned into her old duffel bag. She'd sold all her high-end luggage long ago, though she hated remembering the reason.

By the time she'd packed everything, including a few snacks and water for the road, her shoulders twanged with tension.

Lugging everything she could, she dashed to her Jeep and tossed the bags inside, then hurried back for the rest. Though they'd traveled light from Kansas City, they'd added too many things in their comfortable stay with Ms. Bea.

Back inside the house, she scribbled a quick goodbye note, propped it on Ms. Bea's desk and then called, "Ryder, Paisley, come on. Time to go."

No answer.

She raced to the top of the stairs. "Ryder. Come on. I'm ready."

Still no answer.

Rushing from room to room, she called their names.

Nothing.

Irritation combined with anxiety, ratcheting higher than the puff pastry she'd baked this morning.

*Don't think about that. Don't think about how much you'll miss the bakery and Ms. Bea, about how you'll die a little to leave Bowie.*

Think about protecting the kids.

It was better if no one knew where she'd gone.

Racing from room to room and back downstairs, she looked in every closet, under beds and behind furniture.

"Ryder!" The little scamp was hiding. Where?

The clock over the couch ticked, a reminder that she was running out of time.

"We'll stop for pizza and ice cream," she yelled into the empty kitchen.

A rustling noise came from beneath the kitchen sink.

Under the sink?

*Unbelievable.*

Sage opened the double doors to find two children scrunched tightly inside next to too many toxic chemicals.

Ryder looked up at her. "Is Bowie coming with us?"

If her heart hadn't already been breaking, it would have then. Without answering, she took one hand of each child and tugged them out of the cabinet.

The exit from the house wasn't as easy or as graceful, but she loaded everyone into the Jeep.

As she reached for the ignition key, Ryder leaned forward. "Paisley forgot her lovey."

Of course she did. "Sit tight."

Casting a harried glance toward the end of the street, she loped into the house and returned with the blanket.

As she stepped off the porch, her stomach dropped.

Bowie stood beside her Jeep talking to Ryder, his big black and silver truck parked behind.

The tall cowboy turned to face her.

Every cell in her body begged to go to him and ask him to make everything all right again.

This time he couldn't.

"What's going on?" he asked. "Ryder says you're leaving town."

Mouth dry as bread flour, she nodded. "We have to take a trip."

Bowie blinked, clearly confused. "Now?"

"Yes."

"Where?"

"I don't know."

Uncertainty shifted through his dark eyes and grew like building storm clouds.

"You don't know where you're going? But you have to leave? Just like that? Pardon me if I don't understand. What's going on here, Sage?"

Steeling herself against emotion, she closed her eyes and took a deep breath. She couldn't bear to look at Bowie's worried face, at the suspicion and hurt she saw gathering in his dark eyes.

"When are you coming back?" The words ached from him, deathly quiet and painfully raw.

This was what she'd dreaded. Hurting him.

Yet she was.

Hadn't she warned herself to keep an arm's length between them? For his sake?

She almost sobbed the words. "I can't."

Bowie's broad, dependable shoulders dropped. He was silent for a long throbbing moment while she could almost hear his heart break. Or was that her own?

Guilt and regret and grief wadded together beneath her rib cage with enough pressure to cause an explosion. Her temples pounded until she could barely concentrate.

"Why, Sage? What's happened? I love you. You love me. We talk. We don't do this. Whatever this is."

How did she make him understand that leaving was the best thing she could do for him as well as the kids?

"I can't. We have to leave, that's all."

"Like before? You were going to drive away without a word? After all we've come to mean to each other?"

The pain in his voice threatened her resolve.

She fought off the clawing desire to tell him. He hated druggies. Knowing he'd fallen in love with one would hurt him.

"I wish things could be different. I wish—"

"You're not making any sense. This morning we

planned a celebration. Now, you're running away. Why? What's happened between now and then?"

"I can't tell you."

"You can't or you won't?"

"Both."

"I thought you loved me. Was I that much of a fool?"

"No! I do. If things were different, I'd—" She stopped, though every cell in her body wanted to pour out her love and beg his forgiveness, beg him to love her even though she was not worthy of a man like him.

"Then stop and think. Don't do this to us." His hand swept toward the kids in the back seat. "To them."

She turned her face away, ashamed and scared. "Oh, Bowie, you don't understand."

He was too good. She wasn't.

"Try me. Please. I love you. I love these kids. We can work this out."

His love would die an ugly death if he learned the truth.

The thought of losing him was a hot stab to the throat.

Did he feel the same? Was he suffering because of her?

He'd been abandoned before. Ms. Bea claimed he feared that more than anything.

*Oh, Lord, help me.* I don't know what to do. Am I wrong to leave? Am I hurting this good man all over again?

But what about Ryder and Paisley? Tomorrow Mr. Feldman would know she lied. He'd call the police. The kids would be taken.

What would Bowie think then? He'd been the one to convince Mr. Feldman to trust her. He'd be humiliated, his judgment devalued by the school board, by the whole town.

She couldn't let that happen.

*Tell him. Turn his love to loathing. Set him free.*

*Tell him the shameful truth.*

Gathering all her courage around her like a fortress

wall, she straightened to her full, imposing height. Glancing into the back seat, she hoped the kids couldn't hear her.

Keeping her voice low, she admitted, "I took them, Bowie. I kidnapped the kids. If the authorities find out, I'll lose them forever. I can't let that happen. That's why we have to go."

"What are you talking about? You can't kidnap them. You're their aunt."

"An aunt without any legal standing."

"Okay, let's say that's true." He held his hands out, palms up, pleading. "But that's fixable."

"No, it isn't." Before she let him change her mind, Sage pushed around him and got into the car.

She attempted to close the door. Bowie shoved a boot inside.

"Why not apply for guardianship the way my uncle and aunt did instead of running away? Why do this to them? Or are you just looking for an excuse to move on?" He turned his head aside, fists tight, jaw set. *Wounded.*

He thought she was abandoning him. He thought she didn't want him.

"That's what I'm trying to tell you, Bowie. I can't gain guardianship. Don't you see? I'm…unfit. No judge gives a known drug addict guardianship of two little kids!"

He dropped his foot to the ground. His dark skin blanched. Shock riveted him to the spot. His mouth opened, closed, opened again. "What?"

"You heard me." Slashing a sleeve across eyes that threatened to leak, Sage put the car in Drive. "I was as much a druggie as Amy. Don't love me, Bowie. I'm not worth it."

Now he could hate her. Now he would have no regrets about letting her go.

While he stood there in the cold, stunned and revolted, Sage slammed the car door and drove away.

# Chapter Sixteen

Shocked out of his mind, Bowie moved like a sleepwalker to the porch swing and collapsed.

What had just happened?

His head buzzed. He couldn't think straight.

Sage's words pummeled him like hail stones. She'd kidnapped the children? She was a drug addict?

He shook his head and then dropped it into his hands.

Nothing made sense. Maybe this was a nightmare.

He was so deep in shock that Bowie didn't hear Ms. Bea's minivan pull into the driveway. Nor did he see her approach until she stepped up on the porch.

"Bowie? Everything okay? Where's Sage and the kids?"

He lifted his head. "Gone."

"What?"

"That was my reaction. What and why? She's gone, Bea. Packed up and left." He sighed. "Did you know she's a drug addict?"

Resting her hand on her cane, Bea scoffed. "She is not. Amy is, but not Sage."

Her words echoed in his head. *Don't love me. I'm not worth it.*

"Sage told me herself, right before she drove away."

She'd gutted him with that admission. Why did the two most important women in his life have to love drugs more than him?

"Well, I don't believe it for one minute. I would know. You would too. She's as straight an arrow as you are."

"She doesn't have legal guardianship of Ryder and Paisley either. Says she *kidnapped* them to avoid social services. She thinks no judge will give her guardianship because she's an addict."

"Oh, my." Groaning, the older woman plopped down beside him on the swing. "Poor baby. That's why she came back to Sundown Valley. That's why she was afraid to commit to anything more than temporarily."

"Yeah." Today he'd gone from jubilation to despair all in a matter of minutes. "I love her anyway, Bea."

"I know. She loves you too."

He'd thought so too. She'd even said as much. But, as he'd feared from the beginning, she'd left anyway. He wasn't enough to hold her here.

"Doesn't feel like it at the moment."

Bea clapped an arthritic palm on his knee. "Now, son, don't you go thinking she wanted to leave."

"What else can I believe?" She was restless, always chasing that rainbow, never content.

"Right now, she's running scared. Scared of losing those kids. Scared you'll turn your back on her anyhow, now that you know about the drugs."

"I don't care about her past mistakes." He was a firm believer that when a person gave her life to Jesus, all sins were washed away. Whatever she'd done was cast into God's sea of forgetfulness. She was a new creation in Christ. Didn't she know that?

Bea rocked the swing as she shifted. "She told me the other day she was too happy. She thought the other shoe was bound to drop. Guess it did."

"She said that? That she was happy here and afraid things would fall apart?"

"She sure did. Bowie, honey, Sage has run scared ever since foster care started moving her from placement to placement. When things felt good to her and she'd started to settle in, she was moved somewhere else. Every time. Pretty soon, she left first."

"Before she got hurt again."

"Exactly. The four years she was with Ron and me were the longest, but by then, she'd been disappointed too much. Now, for once in her life, she wanted something so badly that she was willing to take the chance and settle. She wanted this little town for those kids. Most of all, she wanted you."

Could it be true?

Bowie groaned.

What could he do about it now? Sage was gone.

If her phone rang or chirped one more time, she'd be tempted to throw it out the window.

"Aunt Sage, your phone is ringing again."

"I know it, Ryder! I can hear," she snapped.

The back seat went silent.

Regret filtered in stronger than the anxiety.

She pulled to a stop at the edge of town and swiveled toward the back seat. "I'm sorry, buddy. I shouldn't have snapped at you."

Ryder kept his gaze on the toy car in his hands. "Can we go home now?"

She looked from the small boy to his sister.

Paisley watched Sage with the kind of fearful expression she hadn't worn in weeks.

Was she making a mistake?

Was Bowie right? Could they somehow work things out?

But how was that possible? She was not only a recovering drug addict, she was hiding from the authorities.

She reached over the back seat and gripped Paisley's small hand. "It's okay, baby. Don't worry. We'll have fun."

The little bow mouth opened. In a voice as soft as down, Paisley said, "Bowie has fun with us too."

Shocked, amazed to hear the tiny, sweet voice, Sage asked, "What did you say?"

"Bowie was sad. He brought presents."

Ryder turned to stare at his sister, cheeks hot with emotion he struggled to keep in check. "We forgot our Christmas presents. We have to go home."

*Home.* To this precious boy, Sundown Valley was the safe, happy home he'd never had before. Home where Christmas waited. Home where Bowie was sad.

Suddenly, Sage realized how wrong, how twisted her thinking had been.

Love didn't think of itself. Yet, wasn't that exactly what she'd done by trying to leave town a few days before the best Christmas these kids had ever experienced?

She wasn't protecting Ryder and Paisley. She wasn't really protecting Bowie. She'd been afraid of facing her mistakes.

If she truly loved Bowie and these kids, she'd meet her responsibilities head on. All of them.

The kids deserved the stability of Sundown Valley and the love Bowie and Bea and this town offered.

What a foolish thing she'd done.

Would Bowie forgive her? Even if he didn't, he'd stand by these kids. She believed that with everything in her.

Taking her cell phone from the console, she pressed a number. When the phone clicked, she didn't give him time to speak.

"Bowie, if I'm arrested, will you apply for custody of the kids?"

"Yes, but you won't be arrested. I've already called my lawyer."

Something beautiful curled inside her. "You did?"

"Of course I did. I'd do anything for you and those children. Don't you know that by now? Bea says the same. Come home. You have my word. We'll make this right."

"Aunt Sage." Ryder's voice wobbled as he leaned between the seats, beltless again. "A man's only as good as his word. Bowie don't lie. Not ever."

The wise repeat of Bowie's favorite phrase struck Sage between the eyes.

Bowie would move heaven and earth for her and these kids, exactly as she'd rearranged his schedule so he could make his deadline with PJ Enterprises.

That's what love did.

Even if she went to jail, Bowie and Bea would take care of Ryder and Paisley.

She wasn't alone anymore. Hadn't been for months.

Why hadn't she realized that?

Why had she been so afraid to love and be loved?

She looked at the two children belted into the back of her Jeep, longing for home.

Nothing was right about what she'd nearly done. Nothing.

Ryder sniffled. Tears glimmered on his lower lashes.

Paisley's small hand reached for his.

In a whisper Sage knew she'd never forget, the little girl said, "It's okay to cry, bubba. Sage won't put us in a closet."

Sage thought her chest would explode. She pressed the phone against the aching spot. "No, baby. Never ever. No one will ever do that to you again."

She would protect these kids, but she had to do it the right way, even if that meant letting them go.

"Sage? Are you there?"

She raised the receiver to her ear again. "Bowie?"

"Thought I'd lost you."

As always, Bowie was there waiting when she needed him. "I was wrong."

"About?"

"Everything. Can you forgive me?"

"Done."

Sage could scarcely believe how easily he'd said the word. Knowing him the way she did, he meant it.

"I love you, Bowie, so much. I love Ms. Bea and the bakery. I love Sundown Valley. I've just been so ashamed. I never wanted you to know about the bad things in my past."

"The past is the past. Leave it there. Let's talk about the future."

Her heart swelled with love. She didn't deserve him in the least. He loved her anyway. What a fool she was to even consider leaving such steadfast love.

She gazed into the hopeful eyes of two small children who loved this man too.

Slowly, she gave them a wobbly smile and nodded.

"We're coming home. For good. Will you wait for us?"

His relieved sigh rushed over the air waves. "Sage, honey, I've waited for you since I was sixteen. I'll always wait for you. As long as it takes."

# *Epilogue*

On the day of Sage's court date, the skies opened and a cold rain gushed like Niagara Falls from the clouds.

None of the slightly damp gathering cared one iota.

Bowie's lawyer, as promised, had no problem resolving Sage's situation. All that was left was the formality of appearing before the judge and she'd become legal guardian to Ryder and Paisley.

The only thing that made her happier was the man at her side. Every step of the way, he'd been her encouragement, her strength, her love and as always, her very best friend.

Today she was adding Ryder and Paisley to her family. Soon, she hoped to add Bowie too. Not that he'd asked, but she knew he would. The sooner the better as far as she was concerned.

"Miss Sage Walker," the serious judge intoned, causing her heart to jump.

"Yes, sir." She stepped closer to the high bench from which he presided. Bowie came too, finding her hand without looking.

She was glad. Though no one expected this to go wrong, she still suffered a pinch of fear that life really couldn't turn out this well.

She threaded her fingers through Bowie's. Could he feel her trembling?

"Is it your wish to provide for Paisley and Ryder Walker, the children of your incarcerated sister, Amy Walker, as their legal guardian until such time as she is deemed by this court as able and well enough to regain custody?"

Sage glanced at the pair, sitting at the table between the attorney and a social worker, relieved they would not understand the word incarcerated. They'd spoken to their mother by video chat twice. Both times, she'd assured them she wanted them to live with Sage. The kids believed the half-truth that Amy was sick and could not live with them. For now, that was all Sage wanted them to know.

"Yes, sir. Very much so."

"Do you fully understand and embrace all the responsibility that guardianship involves, including financial and emotional needs?"

"I do. I love these children, your honor."

"Let them come up here." Judge Brinker crooked his index finger toward Ryder and Paisley.

Looking like a princess in a frilly pink dress with white tights and shoes and a giant pink bow in her hair, Paisley walked right up. Since finding her voice and the secure life she'd needed, she was gaining confidence in exactly how cute she was. The people at church and in the bakery doted on her something fierce. Sage didn't mind. Paisley needed the attention.

Ryder strutted forward in the navy blue suit he and Bowie had chosen together. He, too, had come a long way in a short time. With extra counseling for both kids and the one-on-one time with Bowie and her, Ryder was blossoming into the charming little boy he should have always been. Today, he'd traded his perpetual frown for a sweet, hopeful expression that melted her heart.

Both children knew what today's court visit meant. They'd been prepped for days.

"Ryder," the judge said, "do you want to live with your aunt Sage?"

"Yes, sir. Aunt Sage treats us real nice. Better than anyone ever did."

Sage glanced at Bowie. He winked. He'd worked with the boy on his manners since the day they'd decided to stay forever.

"Paisley, what about you? Do you like living with your aunt Sage?"

"Yeth, thir." Her little lisp was adorable. "She never has locked us in the closet, and she won't never. She loves us a whole bunches."

The judge didn't bat an eye at the comment. He knew the children's history. He also knew that her speech was a long one for a child who'd hidden her voice for a long time.

"Then I guess all that's left to do is for me to sign these papers." Picking up a pen, he smiled over at Sage and Bowie.

The swirl of joy started building in Sage's middle.

"Sir?" Ryder asked.

The judge turned a surprised eye on the boy. "Yes?"

"Can I bang your hammer?"

A belly laugh erupted from the judge. Sage and Bowie laughed too.

Offering the gavel to the little boy, he said, "Go ahead. Make it official."

And Ryder did.

Bowie hadn't felt this much satisfaction since the day Katherine Pembroke phoned to offer him another, far more lucrative, contract. This time he set the time frame. At present, he refused to give all his hours to the leatherwork. He'd arranged the deadline to reserve plenty of time with Sage and the children too.

Right now, they were his focus.

After a stop next door at the court clerk's office for all manner of stamps and official signatures, they started down the tall steps toward the courthouse exit.

With the children dancing over the concrete foyer like happy bunnies, he pushed open the double doors and stepped outside.

Puddles formed dark spots on the sidewalk. The leafless trees dripped like wet fingers.

"The rain has stopped." Sage, a closed umbrella at her side, reached a hand out. Suddenly, she exclaimed, "Look. A winter rainbow."

Bowie squinted against the sudden burst of January sun to the colors arching over the Sundown Valley skyline.

A rainbow. A sign of God's faithfulness. Could anything, he wondered, be more perfect?

Holding on to one of her hands, he looked at Sage, sincere as he could be.

"Want to chase it?"

A soft smile creased her beautiful face as she shook her head, her green eyes finding his. "I don't need to chase rainbows anymore. I've found my treasure right here in you."

Bowie felt exactly the same.

He'd planned to save this for later, but with the rainbow above, the children grinning up at the adults with such happiness and Sage's words filling his heart, he knew the time was right.

Pausing near a short concrete bench surrounded by an evergreen hedge, he tugged her to a stop.

"Sit." He tossed his jacket over the bench.

Though her expression was quizzical, she did as he asked. The children flanked her, short legs swinging in the chilly air.

This was the perfect spot, though the day could have been warmer.

He wasn't complaining.

He reached inside his shirt pocket, removed the black velvet ring box and flipped it open.

To his great joy, Sage sucked in a delighted gasp.

"Bowie. Yes. Yes!"

He laughed. "Let me ask first."

She stuck out her hand. "Hurry."

He laughed again, thrilled with her reaction as he knelt before her on the wet lawn.

"Sage Walker, I've loved you half my life. Will you settle down with me on Sundown Ranch and love me for the rest of it?"

"No more chasing rainbows," she promised, as he slid the ring onto her fourth finger. "I've found my treasure right here, and it's you. It always was, and I just didn't know it."

"I'm taking that as another yes. I think three does the trick."

Laughing, half crying, which was really unusual, she tugged at his arm. "Get up off that grass before you take pneumonia. And so I can kiss you standing up."

Ryder hopped up too, exclaiming, "You may now kiss the bride."

She wasn't his bride yet. But soon. Very soon.

And so he obeyed the little officiant and kissed her.

He'd no more than raised his head, still gazing into her sparkly eyes, than his cell phone chirped.

"Probably Wade wondering why we aren't there yet." A party celebration waited at the ranch with all their friends. Ms. Bea had even baked a cake.

"Won't they be surprised by this?" Sage held out the sparkling solitaire.

Wade wouldn't be.

He thumbed open the messaging app. "What's this?"

Below a grainy video, Wade had typed, Get a load of this from one of Jinx's cameras. Who does this look like to you?

Expecting to see one of the Keno boys, he tapped the video and let it play.

A tall, very lean form walked directly toward the camera. The gait was odd, but there was something undeniably familiar about the man though his face was mostly obscured behind a long beard and beneath an army-green toboggan cap.

A surge of adrenaline-jacked hope nearly took Bowie's head off. It couldn't be.

He hoped, prayed that it was.

But why would he be hiding in the wilderness? Why not show himself?

"Who is that, Bowie?" She'd leaned in to look at the stranger in the video.

"I think," he said, his heart in his throat, "it's Yates."

"Your cousin?"

"I'm not sure. The video is poor, but yes, I think Yates Trudeau has finally come home."

* * * * *

*Don't miss the next book in* New York Times *bestselling author Linda Goodnight's Sundown Valley miniseries, later this year!*

*And look for the first book in the series,* To Protect His Children, *available now wherever Love Inspired books are sold!*

*Be sure to look for Linda Goodnight's Love Inspired Trade book,* Claiming Her Legacy, *now on sale!*

## COMING NEXT MONTH FROM
## **Love Inspired**

### THE AMISH TWINS NEXT DOOR
*Indiana Amish Brides* • by Vannetta Chapman

Amish single mom Deborah Mast is determined to raise her seven-year-old twin sons *her* way. But when neighbor Nicholas Stoltzfus takes on the rambunctious boys as apprentices on his farm, she'll learn the value of his help with more than just the children—including how to reopen her heart.

### SECRETS IN AN AMISH GARDEN
*Amish Seasons* • by Lenora Worth

When garden nursery owner Rebecca Eicher hires a new employee, she can't help but notice that Jebediah Martin looks similar to her late fiancé. But when her brother plays matchmaker, Jeb's secret is on the brink of being revealed. Will the truth bring them together or break them apart forever?

### EARNING HER TRUST
*K-9 Companions* • by Brenda Minton

With the help of her service dog, Zeb, Emery Guthrie is finally living a life free from her childhood trauma. Then her high school bully, Beau Wilde, returns to town to care for his best friend's orphaned daughters. Has she healed enough to truly forgive him and let him into her life?

### THEIR ALASKAN PAST
*Home to Owl Creek* • by Belle Calhoune

Opening a dog rescue in Owl Creek, Alaska, is a dream come true for veterinarian Maya Roberts, but the only person she can get to help her run it is her ex-boyfriend Ace Reynolds. When a financial situation forces Ace to accept the position, Maya can't run from her feelings...or the secret of why she ended things.

### A NEED TO PROTECT
*Widow's Peak Creek* • by Susanne Dietze

Dairy shepherdess Clementine Simon's only concern is the safety of her orphaned niece and nephew and *not* the return of her former love Liam Murphy. But could the adventuring globe-trotter be just what she needs to overcome her fears and take another chance on love?

### A PROMISE FOR HIS DAUGHTER
by Danielle Thorne

After arriving in Kudzu Creek, contractor and historical preservationist Bradley Ainsworth discovers the two-year-old daughter he never knew about living there with her foster mom, Claire Woodbury. But as they work together updating the house Claire owns, he might find the family he didn't know he was missing...

---